Fox's Feud

Scarface bristled with anger again. 'The whole of this Reserve is my hunting territory,' he seethed. 'From time immemorial my ancestors lived and hunted here, long before it was fenced off by humans, or even had a name. When it was still wild and unchecked countryside, they roamed here freely. And it will always be that way. My cubs will hunt here after me, and their cubs after them . . .'

Fox's Feud

Colin Dann

Illustrated by Terry Riley

RED FOX

A Red Fox Book
Published by Random Century Children's Books
20 Vauxhall Bridge Road, London SW1V 2SA

A division of the Random Century Group

London Melbourne Sydney Auckland
Johannesburg and agencies throughout
the world

First published in 1982
by Hutchinson Children's Books
Sparrow edition 1983
Beaver edition 1985
Reprinted 1987, 1988 and 1989
Red Fox edition 1990
Reprinted 1991

© Colin Dann 1982
Illustrations © Terry Riley 1982

Printed and bound in Great Britain by
Cox & Wyman Ltd, Reading, Berkshire

ISBN 0 09 932260 9

Contents

For Deborah

News

One day during the first spring in White Deer Park, Badger was visited by an excited Mole.

'Badger! Badger!' he called, as he dug his way into the darkness of his old friend's set. 'Have you heard the news?'

'News? News? No, no, *I* haven't heard any news,' replied Badger a little peevishly. He sometimes felt he was a little neglected in his underground home.

'It's Vixen!' declared Mole, beaming. 'She's had four cubs. Fox is so proud! Oh, you should see them . . .'

'When was this?' Badger interrupted. 'Why hasn't Fox been to see me?'

'They were only born last night,' Mole explained. 'Tawny Owl told me all about it. I went to visit them at once. Oh! Badger, you must come. Why don't we go together now?'

'Certainly, if you're sure it would be convenient,' replied Badger. 'Nothing I'd like more.'

'Of course it is,' said Mole. 'Fox instructed me to come and give you the news straight away.'

It was Badger's turn to beam then, and the two animals hastened out of the set, chatting cheerfully.

It was a crisp, sunny spring morning in the Park. A plentiful dew had soaked the ground and each blade of grass and clump of moss glistened refreshingly. Badger sniffed the air briskly. 'It's going to be a wonderful day,' he pronounced.

He and Mole left the little beech copse where Badger had constructed his new set, and directed their steps to another group of trees, in the midst of which lay Fox's earth. In no time Mole's velvet coat was soaked by the dew.

'What a state to arrive in, as a visitor,' he complained. 'Badger, you go on. I must make myself more presentable.'

Badger chuckled and trotted ahead. At the entrance to the earth he paused to listen. There were voices inside. 'Er – hallo,' he called down hesitantly. 'Fox! It's me – Badger. Can I come in?'

The voices ceased for a moment, and then Fox's head appeared at the entrance. 'Badger! How nice to see you. Mole told you the news? We're so thrilled. Come along, old friend.'

Badger followed him down with an expectant smile. He found Vixen curled up on a bed of soft hair, with four tiny, fluffy creatures huddled around her. A warm, truly motherly expression lit up her face. Badger's kind old heart melted at the sight. He was at a loss for words. 'This is a happy day indeed,' he murmured. 'May they have a more peaceful life than we have known.' He looked at Fox.

'Thank you, Badger,' said Vixen quietly. 'I hope so too.'

'Er – will they be foxes or vixens?' Badger enquired a little awkwardly.

'Two male, two female,' Fox replied promptly. 'They'll keep us busy, the four of them, once their eyes have opened.'

'Yes, they certainly look a healthy bunch,' Badger remarked. 'And it's good to see *you* looking so well, Vixen.' He paused. 'Well, I won't intrude too long,' he resumed. 'I expect you want to be on your own.'

Fox made some polite remarks, but Badger was determined not to outstay his welcome.

'I'll come back again, if I may, in a few days,' he promised. Fox accompanied him to the exit.

On his way back to his set, Badger came across Mole basking on top of a hillock in an effort to dry his fur. 'The cubs were all you said they were,' he said to his friend. 'I must admit, on seeing that cosy little group in Fox's earth, I felt a few regrets for a family life.'

'Well, Badger, it's never too late,' Mole said comfortingly. 'You must get lonely in your set, all by yourself.'

'I am at times,' Badger agreed. 'But – no, I'm too old and stubborn in my ways to share my home with any female. I do sometimes feel homesick for my old set in Farthing Wood. Of course, I had my memories there – my family lived there for generations. Here it's different . . .'

Mole cut in quickly before Badger could wax maudlin. 'It's like a new beginning,' he observed. 'The cubs will have their father's characteristics – or some of them. The spirit of Farthing Wood will be renewed – here.'

'Don't get carried away, Mole,' Badger cautioned. 'Farthing Wood will be only a name to them, and life in Farthing Wood as it was for us and Fox and the rest of the band, will be only a story for them to listen to. Here in the Park they'll never know the difficulties and the dangers that were always part of our life there.'

'That's so,' Mole agreed. 'But that's no bad thing, is it, Badger?'

'No – except that, in the face of any danger, they may not be so well equipped for survival.'

Mole pondered this idea for some time, recalling the viciousness of the past winter in the Park. At length he said: 'I'm sure Fox will ensure they will be able to look after themselves.'

Badger smiled. 'What about you, my friend?' he teased. 'You're young. Are you ready yet for a more serious role in life?'

Mole blinked in the unaccustomed brightness of the sunlight. 'I don't often think about it,' he answered. 'But I should like to be settled and happy one day.'

Badger was true to his word and revisited the fox cubs a week or so later. Their eyes were now open and they seemed to be taking a lively interest in everything that went on inside their comfortable earth, which was still the only world they knew. The arrival of Badger was an occasion for the greatest excitement until their father returned with a selection of choice titbits from his evening hunting foray for Vixen. Although the cubs were still suckling, they watched inquisitively as Vixen daintily accepted the food from Fox's jaws.

Badger was amused to see one of them, already slightly larger than his fellows, totter forward to nose at his parents. 'He'll be their leader,' remarked the wise old animal. 'That's plain to see.'

Vixen nodded. 'He'll follow in his father's footsteps.' she remarked. 'The other male cub is not so sure of himself.'

'But the little vixens are charming,' Fox interrupted. 'Just like their mother.'

A noise outside the den attracted their attention. Weasel came towards them out of the early morning daylight.

'There's a strange fox snooping about up there,' he said. 'A big male with a long scar down his muzzle. He seems to be very curious about what might be happening in your den.'

'I've seen him around several times,' Fox said. 'I don't like the look of him, and I've asked Tawny Owl to keep an eye on the den when I'm out hunting.'

'What does he want?' Badger asked with a serious expression.

'I don't know,' replied Fox. 'We may find out one day. He's lived in the Reserve a good number of years – that I do know – and he and his mate have produced many a litter of cubs to populate White Deer Park. I think Vixen and I may be looked upon rather as intruders on his preserve.' All this was said out of earshot of Vixen.

'I asked what his business was here,' Weasel informed his two friends, 'and he replied that the whole of White Deer Park was his business, and who was I to question him?'

'Dear, dear, Weasel, do be careful,' advised Badger, cautious as ever. 'We don't want any misunderstandings with the Park's older residents. Most of them were probably born here, you know.'

'Don't worry about me,' Weasel answered quickly. 'I

keep myself to myself. But I have noticed, since the winter was over, that the acclaim Fox attracted from the residents for his defeat of the poachers seems to have soured slightly.'

'Are we resented, do you think?' Badger asked with a concerned look.

'Not exactly,' replied Weasel. 'But I think there are those here among the Park's original community who feel we ought to recognize our position here as newcomers more clearly than we do. And one of them is our friend Scarface out there.'

'In other words, it's more their home than ours?' Badger summarized.

'Exactly.'

'Well, they accepted us readily enough to begin with,' Fox remarked. 'I don't think there's any real ill feeling. But, I suggest, Badger, we should get everyone together in the Hollow one night soon and talk about the situation. Perhaps it would be as well for us to tread extra warily for a while.'

Badger and Weasel wholeheartedly agreed with Fox's advice and, accordingly, took their leave of Vixen. The scarfaced fox was no longer around when they left Fox's earth and they went their own ways quietly.

Two days elapsed and then all the creatures of Farthing Wood met at dusk in their habitual meeting place in the Hollow.

—2—
Developments

It was the first meeting of all the creatures from Farthing Wood since the winter, and so it was clear to all of them that it was to be of some importance.

'It seems,' began Fox, 'that one or two of you have noticed an undercurrent of – er – unfriendliness running through some of White Deer Park's inhabitants. Now we don't want to find ourselves looked upon as intruders, and I wanted to caution you all to be particularly careful in your behaviour towards the native animals in the future – until things seem quieter again.'

'The Park animals seem to think we have encroached rather on their territory, I believe,' Rabbit remarked.

'That could be true in the case of you rabbits,' suggested Weasel wryly. 'There are so many more of you now than there were when we arrived at the Reserve last summer, despite your losses during the winter.'

Some of the animals laughed but Rabbit was not amused. 'We're not the only ones to have increased our numbers,' he said indignantly. 'What about the hedgehogs? And Toad left his mark in the pond. Even Fox and Vixen now have a family.'

'No offence meant, Rabbit,' Weasel assured him. 'But I think you might have been right about the question of territory. There *are* certain rights respecting that, after all.'

'Humph! Lot of nonsense!' snorted Tawny Owl. 'Plenty of space for everyone. There aren't that many of us.'

'Have you encountered any difficulties, Toad?' Fox asked him.

'No, no,' Toad shook his head. 'Of course, the frogs have known me a long time,' he said, referring to his first visit to the Park. 'They accept me in their pond with the utmost friendliness but, you see, I don't see many of the other creatures. My small legs don't carry me so far as some of you larger fellows.'

The animals chortled at this remark of Toad's, recalling the epic journey he had made alone from White Deer Park across miles of country to return to his home pond in Farthing Wood.

He smiled at their mirth. 'Well, my travelling days are done now, anyhow,' he said. 'I shouldn't relish the prospect of our moving to a third home.'

'No question of it,' Fox assured him hurriedly. 'White Deer Park is our home now. It's a Nature Reserve and we've as much right to be protected as those that were born here.'

'Well said, Fox,' murmured the sardonic Adder, 'and

may I say, from one carnivore to another, I find the irony delicious.'

Fox looked somewhat embarrassed at this unexpected comment, but Badger came to his rescue.

'It's the Law of Nature, Adder,' he reminded him, 'and that is unalterable. We can't all be grass-eaters.'

'Of course not,' drawled Adder, 'especially when there are so much choicer items available.' He leered at the mice, who ignored him totally. They knew perfectly well their common Farthing Wood background meant they were quite safe from the snake's intentions, and that he seemed to feel that such remarks were expected of him.

Hare said: 'My surviving youngster has grown up here. Leveret barely remembers Farthing Wood, so he's far more familiar with the Park's surroundings. The native hares seem to look upon him almost as if he, too, had been born here. He certainly mixes quite freely.'

'I wonder if there are any grounds for apprehension at all,' Kestrel remarked airily.

'Not in your case, certainly,' Vole rasped. 'You spend more time patrolling the countryside outside the Park than you do within its confines.'

'Have you ever thought there might be a reason for that?' Kestrel chided him gently. 'If I always hunted inside the Park, there is a very great danger that some time I might kill the wrong vole or fieldmouse. Small creatures like you look very alike when I'm hovering high up in the sky.'

'That had certainly occurred to *me*,' Fieldmouse assented. 'But, well, you know Vole doesn't always see things so clearly.'

'I must apologize, Kestrel,' Vole said contritely. 'I should have realized you had our interests at heart.'

'Well, well, no harm done,' said Badger the peacemaker.

'Er – is there any more to be said, Fox? This wind is beginning to get very chilly.'

'No more for the present, I think,' said Fox. 'We must all be on our guard for a bit, that's all. I think we should all remain in our corner of the Park for the time being also. That way, if anyone needs to raise the alarm at any time we are in a position to act together quickly.'

At this point Whistler the heron flexed his great wings, producing the familiar shrill sound as the air rushed through the bullet-hole in his damaged one. 'Perhaps a few more of you should have done as I,' he announced in his lugubrious tones, 'and mated with a member of the indigenous population. There can be no swifter way of achieving acceptance amongst a foreign community.'

About three weeks after the meeting in the Hollow, the fox cubs could be seen playing with their parents in the spring sunshine outside their earth. One day Tawny Owl was watching them, sleepily, from a nearby willow tree. He noticed that, although none of them strayed far from a convenient bolt-hole to the den, one cub was slightly more adventurous in his wanderings. His small, chocolate brown body was cobby and healthy looking, as indeed were those of his brother and sisters, but his infant frame seemed to be just a little stouter.

'He's going to be a bold young fellow,' Tawny Owl mused to himself. 'Never still for a moment. Now the others are quite happy to sit at times, and just enjoy the warmth of the sun on their bodies.' He chuckled at their antics. 'Yes, one in particular seems very fond of that.'

Vixen spotted the bird half-dozing on the branch. 'Won't you join us, Owl?' she invited. 'Or are you too sleepy?'.

'Nothing of the kind, nothing of the kind,' Tawny Owl

replied huffily and promptly flew to the ground.

Fox greeted him cheerfully. 'Glad to see you, Owl,' he said. 'Well, it looks as if our fears were groundless. Old Scarface has not been near recently.'

'No. I expect he's occupied in much the same way as you at present,' Tawny Owl observed knowingly.

'Oh? Is he a father again?' Fox asked quickly.

'Oh yes. His mate produced three cubs about the same time as Vixen.'

'Have you seen them?' Vixen wanted to know.

'Not yet,' replied the bird. 'I don't venture over to that section of the Park since our agreement in the Hollow. However,' he added archly, 'I'm sure they couldn't be as delightful as yours, dear Vixen.'

'Oh, flatterer!' she laughed. 'This one we call Charmer actually.' She indicated one of the female cubs. 'She has very winning ways. Her sister is Dreamer.'

'Very appropriate,' agreed Tawny Owl, noticing the cub thus named was the one he had singled out from his perch. 'And the others?'

'The big male cub is Bold,' Fox told him with more than a hint of pride in his voice. 'But we haven't as yet found anything quite applicable to describe his brother.'

'I daresay it'll suggest itself before long,' said Tawny Owl.

'Oh yes,' Vixen agreed. 'They all have their own personalities.'

At that moment the cub in question chose to investigate the family's visitor and approached the owl, wagging his little tail.

'Already as big as me,' Tawny Owl said with amusement. The little cub sat down directly next to him and commenced to sniff him all over. Finally he lay down over Tawny Owl's talons and sighed deeply.

'I think this one's just named himself,' the owl

remarked. 'At any rate, I shall call him Friendly.'

'An excellent name,' Fox assented. 'Don't you think so, dear?'

Vixen nodded happily. There seemed to be nothing that could disturb the peace of such a perfect day. For a while longer Tawny Owl watched the cubs playing and then, finding it increasingly difficult to stifle his yawns, he made an excuse and flew back to his tree for a long nap before dark.

At dusk he awoke with a start to see a familiar shape skulking in the shadows. The scarfaced fox had evidently decided to resume his reconnaisance.

'What on earth is he up to?' Tawny Owl muttered to himself, as he watched the animal pause at one of the entrances to Fox's earth. 'He's listening for something, I'll be bound.'

The beast stood motionless, head cocked at an angle, for some moments. Then he sniffed carefully all round the entrance and listened again. Finally he moved slowly off into the darkness.

Tawny Owl was puzzled. 'Very curious,' he commented.

He was still cogitating when Fox emerged from the earth and paused while he, too, sniffed the air. Then he looked up towards the willow. 'Are you there, Owl?' he called.

'Yes.' Tawny Owl alighted on the ground beside him.

'Have you seen anything?' Fox asked him.

'Scarface has been back.' Tawny Owl described his movements.

'I knew it. I smelt him.'

'He must have detected *your* scent,' Tawny Owl surmised, 'and then decided to go back.'

'Exactly. Had I been out hunting . . .' The friends exchanged glances.

'You can rely on me,' declared Tawny Owl. 'I'll see no harm's done.'

'But, with all due respect, would you be a match for such a tough customer?' Fox queried hesitantly.

'Vixen and I together could deal with him, if necessary,' the bird assured him. 'And, in any case, it may not come to anything. Perhaps it's just harmless curiosity?'

'Perhaps,' said Fox. 'But I don't like it. His secretiveness . . .'

'Are you hunting tonight?' Tawny Owl asked him.

'No. I'll stay put this time. But tomorrow I must. And then . . .?'

'Maybe we'll learn a little more about our interested visitor,' said Tawny Owl coolly. 'As for now, I think I'll pay a call on Badger. We don't want him to feel he's being left out of anything.'

— 3 —

A Warning

The next night was clear and crisp, with a bright half moon. Tawny Owl was in position on the willow branch well before dark, and Badger joined him at the foot of the tree, concealed in a clump of bracken.

When it was quite dark, Fox quitted his earth to go hunting. He gave no sign of any kind that he was aware of his friends' presence. They saw him trot nonchalantly away in the moonlight.

For some time all was quiet. Badger shivered once or twice in the chill evening air and wished he could move about a bit. Neither he nor Tawny Owl spoke. A breeze began to whisper through the leaves of the willow, and with it another faint sound – a regular pattering sound.

Footsteps! Badger tensed under the bracken. The noise came nearer . . . pitter patter, pitter patter . . . and then a long, dog-like shadow was visible on the ground. The pattering ceased. Out into the moonlight came the scarfaced fox, treading very slowly and carefully towards the main entrance to the cubs' den.

By the opening he stopped again and looked all round warily, snuffling the air. For a moment he looked towards the spot where Badger was hidden. The moon shone full on his face, scarred and hideous from a score of battles. Despite himself, Badger's stout old heart missed a beat. Then the animal turned again and lowered himself to creep stealthily into the hole.

At once, Tawny Owl glided noiselessly down from his perch, and Badger rushed forward. Scarface sprang back.

'You've no reason to go in there,' said Tawny Owl. 'What exactly is your game?'

'I'm not accountable to you,' snarled the fox, angry at being detected unawares.

'But you're accountable to the inhabitants of the den who, to my knowledge, have not invited your presence.'

'A social call from one fox to another is no concern of a bird's,' Scarface sneered.

'It is in this instance,' Tawny Owl informed him calmly, 'as I was specifically requested to keep watch for intruders.'

'Intruders?' snapped Scarface. 'Intruders? How dare you talk to me of intruders. I've lived in this Park all my life – *and* my kind with me. I've more right to enter this earth than those who are already in it – cubs or no cubs.'

'Just because you were born here doesn't mean you own the Park, you know.' Badger spoke for the first time. 'There's more than enough room for everyone to live comfortably without any interference being called for. *We* all lost our original homes thanks to human intervention, and we came here for the very reason that it was safe from human hands.'

'Yes, yes, we've all heard about your heroic journey from Farthing Wood,' the fox said sarcastically. 'I was at the reception party when you arrived, just like everyone else. The Park could absorb *your* numbers rightly enough. But now you've started breeding . . .'

'Some of us have,' Badger corrected him. 'I myself have no mate. Neither does Tawny Owl here. But you've nothing to fear from our party. We like to keep ourselves to ourselves.'

'You have to eat, don't you? I'm sure you don't leave the Park every time you go hunting.'

'Of course not,' replied Tawny Owl imperturbably. 'Do you?'

Scarface bristled with anger again. 'The whole of this Reserve is my hunting territory,' he seethed. 'From time immemorial my ancestors lived and hunted here, long before it was fenced off by humans, or even had a name. When it was still wild and unchecked countryside, they roamed here freely. And it will always be that way. My cubs will hunt here after me, and their cubs after them . . .'

'And so on ad infinitum,' Tawny Owl remarked drolly.

Scarface looked at him dangerously, baring his fangs. Badger quailed slightly, though Tawny Owl stood his ground. In slow, menacing tones Scarface said: 'No other family of foxes will be allowed the freedom of the Park. Tell your gallant leader to stay in his own quarter if he values the safety of his mate and her cubs. My family is large: I have many dependents. Don't let him think he can outwit me. I've lived many years and I've yet to be bested.' With a final snarl, he loped off into the shadows.

'Well, well, well,' Badger whispered, 'what an alarming character.'

'Pooh, nonsense,' blustered Tawny Owl, who was secretly shaken by their confrontation, 'nothing but idle threats. We thwarted his little game all right. I believe he was about to do some mischief to Vixen's cubs.'

'I'm sure of it,' agreed Badger. 'But I'm not convinced we've seen the last of him. I have an unpleasant feeling you and I have made an enemy for ourselves tonight, Owl.'

Tawny Owl stretched his wings and shook his feathers in an effort to hide a distinctly disconcerted expression. 'Oh, I don't know . . .' he began.

'Sssh, here's Fox back,' Badger interrupted him. He quickly acquainted Fox with the recent events. Fox invited them down into his earth while he took food in to Vixen. They all sat silent for a while.

'I shall do exactly as he asks,' Fox announced finally.

'What!' exclaimed Tawny Owl.

'Yes, Owl. Vixen and the cubs must be my first consideration. I won't do anything to put their lives at risk.'

'Quite right, my dear fellow,' Badger concurred. 'I should do exactly the same. That creature has a very vicious look about him.'

'And when the cubs are fully grown?' Tawny Owl prompted.

'Well . . . then it might be time to think again,' Fox said cautiously.

'You know you can always count on our support in any way,' said Tawny Owl.

'I know, and I thank you for it, just as I thank you for dealing with that villain just now. But this is my quarrel. I don't want to involve others.'

'Any quarrel of yours is our quarrel too, you know, Fox,' Badger reminded him. 'Remember the Oath we all took before we left Farthing Wood.'

'Of course I remember,' replied Fox. 'But that Oath was sworn to ensure the mutual protection of all our party while we were on our journey. We've made new lives for ourselves here – all of us. I don't want to endanger my friends for any selfish reason.'

'Well, I think in the event of any trouble,' Badger opined, 'you will find that everyone will get involved, whether you request it or not. Our ties are more lasting than simply for the duration of a journey.'

'That is indeed a comforting thought, Badger, my dear friend,' said Fox who was evidently quite moved. 'And Owl – what a true friend you've been.'

'Oh, don't mention it,' Tawny Owl said self-consciously. 'Glad to be of assistance, I'm sure.'

Just then Vixen, who had finished eating, came forward. 'Fox told me the gist of what occurred tonight,' she said, 'and I want to thank you both for standing guard as you did. If you look at the cubs, you can see how successful you were.'

They could see them blissfully asleep in a huddle, completely unaware of the interest provoked by their existence.

'They'll soon be big enough for me to take them hunting,' she added. 'They're coming along fast.'

'Yes, yes, they grow so quickly,' said Badger fondly. 'It's a shame in a way. But they need to be able to stand on their own feet as soon as possible.'

'Never more so than in the present case,' Tawny Owl remarked, but Fox gestured him to silence.

'Well, it's been an eventful evening,' he summarized. 'Owl, Badger, I'm sure you both feel the need to eat. We'll keep in touch.'

Badger took this as a hint that Fox wanted to be alone with his family and began to amble towards the exit, but the somewhat insensitive Owl lingered.

'No hurry, no hurry,' he said. 'My stomach takes second place to the pleasure of your company.'

'Now, we mustn't outstay our welcome,' Badger said pointedly. 'Fox has other claims on his time.'

Tawny Owl noticed his gaffe but endeavoured to appear unconcerned. 'Of course,' he said, 'I just wanted to make it quite clear I was not in any discomfort.'

Badger had already made his farewells and left the earth.

'I'll be on watch again tomorrow evening,' Tawny Owl assured Fox awkwardly. 'Never fear.'

Fox smiled. 'All right, Owl. Thank you.'

Tawny Owl cleared his throat. 'Well – goodbye,' he finished lamely, and finally left them alone.

— 4 —

First Blood

The time came when the four cubs were ready to go on their first hunting trip. Many of Fox's and Vixen's friends came to witness this important outing, among them Badger, Mole, Weasel and, of course, Tawny Owl. It was dusk as they gathered outside the earth, and watched Vixen shepherd Bold, Charmer, Dreamer and Friendly towards the entrance.

The cubs emerged with various degrees of enthusiasm. Bold looked keen and alert; his robust young body was tingling with excitement. Charmer stayed close to her mother, watching her every movement, but Dreamer, as usual, seemed to be in a world of her own – wandering off to sniff at a patch of grass or a twig as if she had all the time in the world. Friendly made a beeline for the onlookers, wagging his tail furiously as he recognized each of them in turn.

Vixen called them together again and had a few last words with Fox, who impressed on her once more not to attempt to hunt outside their own corner of the Park. She took a necessarily quiet farewell of him and of their friends and led the cubs away. Shortly afterwards Fox followed, making sure he was out of sight and keeping far enough behind for his scent to remain undetected. For, although it was Vixen's job to instruct the cubs, he was determined to be within reach should anything untoward occur.

'Keep close to me,' Vixen told the cubs, 'and there's no danger. Do you understand, Dreamer? No wandering off!'

'Don't worry, Mother,' the cub replied. 'I'll stay with you.'

Bold was snuffling the night air keenly as the little group trotted on. A hundred exciting scents were wafted to him on the breeze and his young feet fairly danced along in his exhilaration.

'I want complete quietness now,' Vixen ordered, as she led them into some long grass. Friendly, who had been chatting to his sister cubs, fell silent. They followed their mother in a line, nosing their way through the tall stalks. A variety of insects scattered in their wake – beetles, crickets, spiders and earwigs. Some tumbled into their path, and following their mother's example, they snapped them up. They quickly discerned which were to their liking.

But Vixen was after larger game. They arrived on the banks of a stream rich in water-rats. She showed the cubs how to exercise their patience while nothing seemed to appear; then, when the prey was spotted, to freeze if it approached or, alternatively, to stalk it from behind. She

showed how to pounce and pin it with front paws and
how to render it immobile with the jaws.

The cubs at first were clumsy and too eager, and for a
long time they caught nothing. The water-rats were far
too nimble and knowing for them. But Bold caught a
water-shrew at the stream's edge and this success spurred
him on. Vixen helped the others and, eventually,
Charmer and Friendly were also successful. Only
Dreamer, who had eaten rather too many insects and
earthworms on the way, showed little aptitude.

'You will go hungry tonight,' Vixen told her. 'Then
tomorrow perhaps you will try harder.'

All the time Fox watched them from further downstream.
When he saw they were about to leave he disappeared.
He was satisfied that there was no danger abroad and that
they would soon be safely back in the den again. He had
completely failed to notice a familiar figure, hidden in the
shadows on the opposite bank. Scarface had also been
watching the cubs' lesson, but from a quite different
motive.

At that very moment in another area of the Park his
mate was going through the self-same procedure with her
cubs. Scarface looked with anger and resentment at
Vixen's cubs, comparing his own unfavourably with
them. Vixen's seemed sturdier and more agile. In reality
only Bold was bigger, but he likened the cub's brother
and sisters to him in his mind's eye. He jealously watched
Bold's dawning skills and knew that he could be supreme
among all the foxes one day. 'But that shall not be,' he
muttered darkly to himself. 'No interloper will supercede
me and mine while I live. This young cub must be dealt
with before he grows any more.'

He watched Vixen set off with the cubs following, and
then swam across to the other bank silently. As they re-
entered the long grass, he ran quickly round the outside

to head them off. Vixen emerged first, then Charmer and Dreamer, and finally the two male cubs. Scarface set up a loud yapping and barking to startle them. Vixen halted stock still, but all four cubs leapt into the air in alarm. She saw the hostile fox speeding towards them.

'Quickly!' she cried. 'Run for the earth!'

The cubs set off as swiftly as their legs could carry them, while their mother faced about to encounter their attacker. But Scarface twisted out of her reach and raced after her young ones. In no time his longer legs brought him up to their heels. He knew he would have time only to catch one cub, and he immediately singled out Bold for attack. Running in amongst the cubs, he scattered them and isolated Bold by shielding him with his body. Then he bared his fangs and prepared to lunge.

But Bold was not so named for nothing. Taking Scarface completely by surprise, the plucky little animal snapped at the old fox first, and bit him neatly on the foreleg. Scarface actually fell back a pace or two in utter amazement at the cub's audacity. For a moment he was dumbfounded; then, with a wild snarl, he sprang forward again.

By now Vixen, with her famed swiftness, was catching up with the aggressor. As she ran, she let out a piercing scream as a signal to Fox. The eerie cry cut through the night air like a knife, and was heard not only by Fox but by a number of the other Farthing Wood animals.

Before Scarface could aim again at Bold, Vixen was in between them, snapping viciously at the hideous muzzle while she protected her bravest cub. The other three were now out of danger and well on the way back to their den. While Vixen and Scarface lunged and feinted at each other, growling horribly the whole time, Bold ran round his mother and bit his enemy from behind with his sharp young teeth.

Scarface was in a fury – the attacker became the attacked. As he swung backwards and forwards, he spied in the distance Fox galloping in their direction. He knew it was time to break off the contest. With a final wild snap at Vixen which caught her a glancing blow on the shoulder and made her yelp, Scarface broke free and made off at a good pace back to his own kind.

Fox saw this as he approached and felt inclined to race after him, but Vixen's cry of pain had decided him to attend to his family first. He was quickly assured when it became obvious Vixen had only sustained a scratch. While he comforted his mate, Fox said: 'That creature is beginning to interfere a little too much in our affairs. If he wants to really stir up trouble, I'll give him something he didn't bargain for.'

'He was after Bold,' panted Vixen. 'I don't know why – the other cubs didn't interest him.'

'Where are they?' Fox asked quickly.

'They got away, luckily. They should be back in the den by now.'

Fox sighed with relief and then smiled down at Bold, who was wagging his tail as hard as he could, begging for recognition.

'You're a game one,' his father said to him. 'I saw you helping your mother.'

'He was defending himself before I came on the scene,' Vixen told him. 'He bit that hateful creature before he had a chance to *be* bitten.'

'No, did he though?' Fox murmured. 'What, he attacked old Scarface?' There was pride in his voice. 'My word, that *is* something.'

'I thought he was going to kill me,' said Bold quietly, 'so I had to do *something*.'

'Well, you certainly seem to be able to look after yourself,' Fox praised him. Yet, even as he spoke, in his heart he knew the brave little cub would from now on be the prime target for their enemy – even more so than before. Scarface would never forget his humiliation of this night.

Fox made Vixen tell him in detail exactly what had happened from the time he let her out of his sight. 'So he's not even true to his word,' he muttered afterwards. 'We *have* kept to our own area, and still he has sought us out. Well, now we know where we stand for sure.'

They heard a familiar voice calling them. 'Fox! Vixen!' It was Badger. He ran up to tell them that the other cubs were safely in their earth, in the care of Weasel and Mole. Then he stopped in dismay, looking down at Bold. 'But where's Dreamer?' he asked.

'What?' gasped Vixen. 'Wasn't she with the others?'

'No, only Charmer and Friendly are in the den. We thought she was with you.' Badger looked almost as worried as the parents.

'Then wherever can she . . .?' began Fox.

'She's wandered off somewhere again,' Bold said. 'She's always doing that. I'm sure she'll be all right, Mother,' he added comfortingly.

'We must search for her,' said Fox. 'Badger, will you take Bold back to join the others?'

'Of course, Fox. Anything I can do – you know that.'

Fox and Vixen split up to comb different areas, calling softly to their lost cub. Inside the earth, the three other cubs and their guardians waited anxiously.

It was Fox who found her. Vixen heard his cry – an angry, baffled cry of distress. She found him standing over the body of Dreamer. She was dead, and her young body had been badly savaged.

There was no doubt in their minds who had done the deed. Fox's face was very grim. With menace he said: 'Now indeed he will have a fight to contend with.'

— 5 —

Out of Bounds

The savage killing of an innocent cub was a considerable shock to the Farthing Wood community. There were those who thought it should be avenged, while others advised greater caution. Amongst the smaller animals there was widespread alarm. They had thought themselves safe and now it appeared there was a new threat to their lives.

The strongest advocates of taking revenge for the death of Dreamer were the birds – Tawny Owl, Kestrel and Whistler. Fox, however, was wise enough to recognize that, in the event of a prolonged state of conflict, they stood to suffer least. Their wings were their constant passport to safety. For a long time he brooded over what course of action to take. Vixen's grief was an aching wound in his heart, and he itched for battle. But he did not want to further endanger the survival of his other three cubs. So for the time being Scarface's blow remained unanswered.

Over the next few weeks the cubs were never allowed to wander far, and at night both Fox and Vixen accompanied them on their hunting trips. Soon the three were very nearly as big as their parents and Bold, in particular, was wishing to become more independent. It was Vixen who finally said to Fox: 'We can be overprotective, you know. Shouldn't we be encouraging them to rely more on themselves now?'

'I suppose you're right,' Fox acknowledged. 'But do you think they're ready to meet *all* the dangers around?'

'Time will tell,' said Vixen realistically. 'In any case, the dangers you are referring to will always be present. The cubs are aware of them, too.'

Fox relented. 'I'll tell them they're free to go where they choose, but within reason. We don't want to invite trouble.'

The next day Fox and Vixen hunted alone, and the cubs were left to their own devices. Bold was eager to explore further afield and, before he left them, he made Friendly and Charmer promise not to mention this.

With what sense of freedom and adventure he set off in the moonlight! His natural confidence made him feel he was equal to anything and he trotted along quite fearlessly. He went first to the stream of the water-rats and slaked his thirst at its edge. He had never been to the other bank and, without further ado, dog-paddled easily across. Here there were new smells, new sounds to absorb. Bold watched an owl flitting from tree to tree, calling in its metallic voice to its mate. A stoat brushed in front of him, intent on its own business. Bold caught himself a morsel and paused to eat it under a birch tree.

'Hallo,' whispered a voice nearby. 'I don't think I know your face.'

Bold looked around him and detected a movement under a gorse bush. He looked closer. 'Oh – hallo,' he said in reply. 'You must be Adder.'

'That is the case,' said the snake.

'My father has often talked to me about you,' Bold went on.

'Really? What did he say?'

'He said you were a remarkable creature,' Bold said innocently.

Adder chuckled. 'Not so remarkable for a snake,' he said. 'But it seems we legless individuals always appear unusual to those who have them.'

'I don't think he was referring to that aspect at all,' Bold assured him. 'My father and mother have good cause to remember some of your deeds.'

Adder knew the young fox was referring in particular to a certain action on his part during the animals' journey to White Deer Park, when he had virtually saved Vixen's life. But it was not his way to acknowledge it. 'I'm glad to hear it,' was all he said. 'For my part, I have the greatest admiration for your parents. Incidentally, I trust I am not delaying you at all?'

Bold was much too polite to say he had wanted to explore alone, and he thought Adder was a particularly interesting character to whom he might do well to listen. 'I should be glad of your company,' he said, more or less truthfully.

'I heard, of course, of the tragic incident involving your sister,' Adder told him. 'It seems there are certain rivalries in existence in the Park. I must say I have been surprised at the somewhat subdued response from your father. At one time he would have reacted quite differently – but then he hasn't always had the particular responsibilities he has had recently.'

Bold was surprised at the snake's outspoken manner, but he recalled that Fox had told him that Adder had never been one to mince his words.

'I'm sure if that scarfaced animal ever came close to our den again, my father would kill him,' the cub said proudly.

'Ye-e-s,' drawled Adder, 'possibly. The only drawback is that, if he did return, he might not be unaccompanied.'

'Neither is my father unaccompanied,' Bold answered hotly. 'I'm nearly as big as he is, and I would certainly not see him fight alone.'

Adder grinned wryly. 'I don't doubt it for a moment,' he assured the cub. 'You youngsters are bound to be eager to prove yourselves.'

Bold felt the snake was amused at his ardour, but for once Adder had not intended to be sarcastic, and hastened to reassure him.

'I should know that any offspring of Fox and Vixen would be bound to have a stout heart,' he said.

This compliment both to himself and his parents flattered the cub.

'Er – were you spying out the land by any chance?' Adder enquired.

'Not exactly,' replied Bold innocently. 'I just wanted to explore a little further than before.' He did not care to admit that he was out on his own for the first time.

'The only reason I asked,' resumed the snake, 'is that I know Scarface and his brood patrol these parts.'

Bold swallowed hard. Despite his determination to be courageous, he was not yet ready to face the enemy on his own. 'Oh,' he said quietly. 'Er – do they cover a lot of ground?'

Adder saw how the land lay. 'Oh, a great deal,' he replied, a hint of his old maliciousness creeping into his feelings. 'They seem to feel they have the right to roam wherever they choose.'

These words caused Bold to shake off his trepidation. 'And why shouldn't I, too?' he said with resolution.

'No reason at all,' Adder consented, wondering if he was wrong to spur the cub on. 'Feel free to go. I've no wish to hold you back.'

Now Bold felt that he must go on. He turned to Adder. 'I'm grateful to you for your advice,' he said politely. 'Will you be in this vicinity for some time?'

'Oh, hereabouts,' Adder replied non-committally.

'Well then, if I don't return this way tonight, will you seek out my father and tell him?'

Adder loathed to be given commissions of any sort, or to feel himself bound in any way by the wishes of others. He was on the point of delivering a retort, but confined himself to pointing out that he might be moving on anyway.

'I know Fox would appreciate it,' Bold urged him.

Unwittingly, the cub had probably chosen the one motive that struck a chord in Adder's scaly old heart. He owned few allegiances, but Fox commanded one of them.

'You may count on me,' he said simply.

Bold made his farewells and trotted forward carefully, sniffing the air in every direction as he did so. The hairs of his coat seemed to stand up independently as, with every step, he felt he was penetrating deeper into alien territory. Pretty soon, he was sure he detected the smell of a fox. He instantly flattened himself against the ground and waited.

The smell strengthened. He heard the sound of fox paws on the ground. A young fox came into view, pausing every so often and sniffing the air cautiously, just as he had done. He saw the other cub look all around as if trying to pinpoint him.

Bold realized he had nothing to fear. The other cub was just as nervous of their encounter as he was, and also far less robust in his appearance. He got to his feet quietly and waited.

The other cub spotted him and was startled. He even backed a couple of paces instinctively, snarling as he did so.

'I mean no harm,' Bold said clearly. 'I'm merely looking around.'

'Well, you shouldn't be looking around here,' the other cub said sullenly. 'You're no relation of mine, and we don't allow strangers in our domain.'

'But you've no objection, apparently, to venturing into theirs?' Bold answered.

'You're one of the Farthing Wood creatures,' said the cub. '*That's* your domain.'

'On the contrary,' Bold replied coolly. 'I'm as much a White Deer Park fox as you are. I was born here too, you know.'

The other cub was silenced by this remark.

'What do they call you?' Bold asked in a not unfriendly manner.

'Ranger,' came the reply.

'Well, I'm known as Bold,' said Fox's cub, 'and I would like to ask you: is it necessary for you and I to continue the quarrel of our parents? We might be friends elsewhere. Why not here?'

Ranger said nothing. He seemed about to respond to this gesture of good will, when his father suddenly appeared. With his customary vicious snarl, Scarface got between Bold and his own cub.

'You are going to regret straying from the safety of your family,' he said with measured iciness. 'This will be the first and the last time you enter our boundaries.'

Bold stood his ground, wondering what move was going to be made. He tensed his muscles, ready to spring into flight the moment he had to. He kept an unwavering gaze on the old scarred muzzle of his enemy, ensuring that Ranger also was constantly in his circle of vision.

Ranger, in fact, appeared to be very ill at ease. He kept shifting his weight from one paw to another, looking quickly from his father to Bold and back again.

Scarface suddenly growled impatiently at him, comparing his restlessness unfavourably with the coolness of Bold. Ranger slunk back behind his father. Bold and Scarface continued to eye each other.

In a split second before the old fox launched himself forward, Bold read the intention in his eyes. He leapt nimbly aside and Scarface rushed past him a few yards before he could check himself. Bold faced him again and, this time, as he hurtled towards him Scarface signalled to Ranger to attack Bold's rear.

But Bold was far too supple for one old and one inexperienced fox. He had his father's swiftness and agility. He slid away from the attack and began to run back on his old path, back towards Adder.

With a wild bark of fury and frustration Scarface leapt after him. Ranger followed, more out of a sense of obedience than a desire to do so.

Bold ran easily and confidently, knowing he had the better pace. Then he heard a yelping cry behind him – an eerie wail of a cry, repeated over and over again. He quickened his pace, knowing Scarface was calling to his own kind for assistance.

Bold raced on – it was all he could do. Then, some yards ahead, he saw a flurry of movement. At the sight his blood ran cold. About a dozen foxes were running towards him, spreading out in an arc to encircle him.

Behind him Scarface's gasps rasped in his ears. He knew his case was hopeless. The other foxes surrounded him and halted his progress. Silently they awaited the arrival of their sire.

Bold looked fearfully from one pair of eyes to another. They were full of intent. There was no mercy in any of them.

—6—
Some Support

Adder, who had been watching during the remainder of the night for Bold's return, felt the first rays of the summer sun strike his body with their warmth. He knew it was time to report the cub's absence.

Slithering as quickly as he was able through the bracken and leaf litter, he arrived at the stream-bank. Adder was a good swimmer and the stream presented no problems. He forded it easily, and climbed the other bank. But Fox's earth was a good distance away and Adder knew it would be hours before he could reach it. His body was not constructed to travel long distances at speed. It was essential for him to find someone who could pass the message more quickly.

He knew of no Farthing Wood animal who had set up

home in the immediate vicinity. Kestrel would be the perfect messenger, but there was no way in which Adder could pass it to him hundreds of feet up in the air, even should he be flying over the Park. He might encounter one of the other birds, but Tawny Owl was likely to be asleep, while Whistler spent most of his time at the waterside. But the heron was not always to be found along the banks of the stream and Adder could spare no time on what might prove to be a fruitless search. So he struggled on overland.

As luck would have it, as his mosaicked body rippled through the long grass, he came upon Hare resting on his form of flattened stalks.

'*You* don't often pass this way,' Hare said.

'There's a reason for it,' Adder told him, and explained the urgency of the message. 'It's a definite stroke of luck running into you. You've probably got the fastest pair of legs in the whole Reserve.'

Hare did not hesitate. He was up and bounding away through the grass without so much as a farewell. Adder found himself a warm patch of ground and decided to do some basking. He was sure events would catch up with him again later in the day.

Minutes later, Hare's breakneck speed brought him to the entrance to Fox's earth. Inside he found Fox and Vixen, Friendly and Charmer already deeply concerned at Bold's failure to reappear. When they received the news that he had deliberately strayed into Scarface's territory, they conjectured the worst.

Fox looked strained. 'We must go after him at once,' he resolved. 'It may not be too late.'

'I'll go and alert Badger and some of the others,' Hare offered.

'No.' Fox shook his head. 'I've said this before and I'll say it again. This is mine and Vixen's quarrel. We'll deal with it ourselves. I don't want any of our friends getting hurt on our account.'

'Very well,' said Hare. 'But if you need help, it would be absurd not to ask for it from any reason of pride.'

'There are four of us here,' Fox indicated his family. 'Friendly and Charmer are all but fully grown. We will go, as a pack, to search for our missing one.'

'We won't be looking for any trouble,' Vixen added. 'We don't want any fighting. Our only concern is to find Bold and bring him back.'

'I wish you well,' said Hare sincerely.

'Thank you for bringing us word,' said Vixen. 'We may be able to thank Adder ourselves.'

Hare watched the family depart. He had little confidence, either that they would find Bold or, if they did, be able to bring him away, and all of them return unscathed right from under the muzzle of Scarface. In the sunlight again, he sat pondering. He did not care to defy Fox's wishes, yet he knew Badger and Tawny Owl, at least, would never forgive him if he did not warn them of the developments.

'I suppose all I can do is to pass on to them Fox's words,' he said to himself, 'and hope that they'll respect them.' He pondered again. 'Of course Tawny Owl is bound to act impulsively, as usual. Perhaps I'll just tell Badger.'

Having decided this, Hare ran quickly to Badger's set and found him entertaining Mole. He described the situation in a few words.

'I *knew* they were going to have problems with that one,' Badger said afterwards. 'But, after all, he's not really a cub any more. He has a life of his own now. Of course, the maturity isn't there . . .'

'Oh, why won't Fox let us help him?' bewailed Mole.

'I'm sure Scarface would respect the combined forces of all the animals of Farthing Wood.'

'A lot of you are so small as not to influence his thinking in any way, *I'm* sure,' Badger remarked. 'No offence, Mole, you understand. But an old warrior like Scarface is hardly likely to take much account of you or Vole – or Toad, for that matter. He's quite capable of making a tasty morsel of you for his supper.'

Mole looked a little hurt. 'Well, my intentions are noble enough, anyway,' he defended himself. 'But there's a lot to be said for numbers.'

'I think Mole's right, actually,' Hare agreed. 'Most of the creatures in the Park still think there's a certain aura about us. We made that famous journey – against all odds. We are looked upon as being exceptionally resourceful – why should we be intimidated by any danger that confronts us here after all we endured before?'

'That's it exactly!' cried Mole. 'I couldn't have put it better myself.'

'The only thing being,' Badger reminded them, 'that we are required not to get involved.'

'I suppose Fox wouldn't have any objection if we just followed along behind at a safe distance?' Hare queried. 'You know – just to satisfy ourselves everything was all right?'

Badger looked at Mole knowingly. 'What do you think, Mole?' he asked.

'Oh, I shouldn't think there could be any complaint about that,' he surmised.

'Then we'd better leave at once,' Badger said immediately. They had found the excuse they needed.

'We'll collect Weasel on the way,' he said. 'And as many of the others as possible.'

Hare voiced doubts about Tawny Owl.

'Oh no, we can't leave Owl out,' Badger said loyally. 'You leave him to me. He won't do anything rash, I'm sure.'

Mole took up his old travelling position on Badger's back and the three animals set off. Weasel made the party four in number and then the ranks were later swelled by Hedgehog, Rabbit and Squirrel. Tawny Owl was soon located and they all had a welcome surprise when Kestrel came swooping down towards them, having spotted the party from the air.

'I thought something was afoot,' he remarked when Badger had explained all. 'I'll fly on ahead and see if I can find Fox and family.'

The animals felt something of their old spirit of camaraderie returning as they went along, and they recalled their many adventures together on their long journey to the Park. At that time they had been united by a common desire to reach safety in a new home. Now, again, they had joined together in a new crisis. The safety of their old leader, Fox, in the *new* home was threatened and it was their duty to support him.

They arrived at the spot where Adder had encountered Hare, but the snake was no longer to be seen.

'He's probably concealed himself somewhere,' suggested Weasel. 'Adder was never one to admit to a community spirit. He always preferred an individual approach.'

'But he was never one to be found wanting in times of danger,' Badger asserted. 'I shouldn't be surprised if he isn't accompanying Fox and Vixen. They must have passed this way.'

The return of Kestrel brought them further news. 'Fox and Vixen are on the other side of the stream,' he told them, 'with the two other cubs. They've seen and heard nothing and they are proceeding very cautiously indeed.'

'Was Adder with them?' Mole enquired.

'No. No sign of him,' the hawk replied.

'He's probably sleeping somewhere like the sensible creature he is,' Tawny Owl observed and yawned. 'Best thing to do when the sun's up.'

'Adder never *really* sleeps,' said Mole. 'Not like we do. He's got no eyelids.' He giggled.

'We all have our own features, Mole,' Badger pointed out. 'Adder might make a joke of your short-sightedness.'

Mole fell silent. He had been touched on a raw spot.

Tawny Owl was still yawning. 'Dear me,' he remarked. 'I didn't realize I was so tired. Perhaps I should have carried on dozing. I probably won't be of much use.'

'I don't know whether any of us will be of use,' returned Badger. 'Fox doesn't want us to interfere. It's really only a case of giving moral support.'

They moved on to the stream and swam across in a line, Kestrel and Tawny Owl flying overhead. Once on the other bank they fell silent. The feeling that they were entering hostile territory came over them very strongly.

Rabbit whispered: 'Do you think there's a lot of point in our continuing? I mean, this area is patrolled by that hideous scarfaced fox and his family and – well, Hare and I are their natural prey.'

'You mean there's no point in *your* continuing,' Weasel emphasized dryly. 'Well, I suppose support that is given so timidly cannot really be called support anyway.'

'Just a moment, Weasel,' Hare came to his cousin's rescue for once. 'Rabbit has a right to be timid. Hares and rabbits are no match for foxes.'

'We haven't seen any foxes yet,' Weasel reminded him.

'I can smell them,' said Rabbit. 'I feel as if I am walking

right into their waiting jaws.'

'There's a nice thick bank of nettles there,' remarked Tawny Owl. 'Why don't you animals hide yourselves there for a while, and Kestrel and I will do some reconnoitring?'

The animals concurred, and the two birds left them for the time safely concealed.

An eerie stillness pervaded the air – all the animals felt uneasy. Rabbit, most of all, was unable to settle.

'It's like the calm before the storm,' he whispered to Hare nervously.

Squirrel ran up the trunk of the nearest tree on to a lofty branch to 'a point of vantage' as he put it.

Suddenly the sound of running footsteps was heard, approaching quickly. The animals peered out from the undergrowth and were amazed to see none other than Bold racing from the rear of the position they had reached, towards the stream.

Badger hailed him, and the cub halted on the bank. The animals ran towards him in a group.

'I escaped,' he panted. 'I'm too fast for them.' His shoulder was a little bloody. Bold discounted it. 'There was a bit of a scuffle,' he explained. 'Things really looked dangerous for a time. I've run hard – I must have a rest.'

Badger and Weasel led him to the nettle-patch.

'I'll just take a breather,' said the cub, 'and then I'll tell you what happened.'

—7—
The Result of Thoughtlessness

After a minute or two, Bold was more composed. He explained how he had become surrounded by Scarface and his tribe the previous night, and had fully expected they were going to kill him.

Mole gasped. 'How dreadful! What have you ever done to them?'

'Nothing,' replied Bold, 'except humiliate their leader on one occasion. But he has my sister's death on his conscience. He must have thought I had come for revenge.'

'What, against so many?' Badger asked incredulously.

'No, against himself.'

'I hardly think . . .' began Badger. 'I mean, if your father didn't . . .'

'Oh, my father is *too* cautious,' said Bold.

'In the wild,' Weasel pointed out, 'caution is the essence of survival. In the meantime your father and the whole of your family are out looking for you in the alien territory from which you have just escaped.'

'But we must stop them – get them back,' urged the cub.

'How do you propose we do that? Follow them?' Hedgehog enquired. 'We're too small and too few.'

'But *I* was on my own and *I* outwitted them,' Bold reminded him, a trifle boastfully.

'Well, tell us how,' said Hare. 'We're still waiting to hear.'

'Yes. Well, as I told you, I was surrounded. I was lucky it was night-time, for it was also hunting time, and it seemed that hunting was the foxes' priority. Scarface told his henchmen to escort me to an unoccupied earth, which they did. I was then forced inside, while some of the group stood guard at each of the exits.'

'And then?'

'They stayed behind while the others went after their prey.'

'How long were they gone?' Mole asked. 'You must have been terrified.'

'I don't know how long they were gone, because I knew that if I was still in that earth when they got back I would never get out alive. So their hunting was my breathing space. I started to talk to one of the animals left on guard, and managed to persuade him inside. He was not as big as I, and I made a rush at him, baring my fangs. As he sidestepped, I altered my direction in mid-career and bolted out of the exit. Once outside I skipped past the other guards and then I simply ran and ran and ran, knowing my life depended on it.'

'How does your shoulder come to be injured?' Badger wanted to know.

'There was a tussle on my way back. As I was running quite blindly, as fast as I could, I ran across two foxes busy stalking their quarry. One of them made a half-hearted lunge and grazed my shoulder. I don't think I was even recognized. I was just looked upon as a rival for their food supply.'

'Well, you are a remarkably lucky young fellow,' Badger observed, 'to have reached safety again.'

'I think my cunning and fleetness of foot had something to do with it,' Bold retorted.

Not for the first time Badger detected the note of boastfulness in Bold's remarks.

'Perhaps so, perhaps so,' he conceded. 'But because of your rashness in coming to this area in the first place you have put the lives of your family in danger and, to a lesser extent, ours also.'

'I'm sure my father will see everyone is quite safe,' Bold maintained.

'But he is groping in the dark, so to speak, isn't he?' Badger remarked. 'He doesn't know where you are, and until he does he will continue to search for you.'

Bold's face dropped a little. 'Can't we send word to him?' he suggested.

'But, you see, we don't know where *he* is. Kestrel and Tawny Owl have gone to find him. But when they do, they still won't know about you, will they?'

'Oh dear,' said Bold. 'I do seem to have caused rather a lot of bother.'

'You must learn to think before you act,' Badger continued sternly. 'That is the caution Weasel was talking about earlier.'

'I take your point, Badger, and I apologize. Can I do anything?'

'I don't see that you can, any more than the rest of us until we're more sure of the situation. We shall just have to wait here until the birds return.'

'I bet there were some recriminations when Scarface returned from hunting and found you gone,' said Mole. 'It's surprising they haven't come searching for you.'

'They must have been diverted by the sudden appearance of Bold's family,' Weasel remarked. 'In any case, they'll probably presume that by now he's safe back in his own territory.'

'I feel so guilty now,' Bold said contritely, 'leading you all into trouble like this.'

'Well, well,' said Badger kindly, 'as long as you learn your lesson from it.'

Squirrel came racing back down the tree-trunk. 'Kestrel's coming!' he called to them as his small body leapt jerkily over the ground. He had scarcely rejoined the party when Kestrel landed beside them. He uttered a cry of amazement when he spotted the fox cub. 'Goodness gracious! How are you come here?'

Badger related Bold's story.

Kestrel glared at the cub angrily. 'There's your father confronting your enemy and demanding your return and all the time you're lying here in safety,' he screeched.

'Where *is* my father?' Bold asked the hawk hastily. 'Is he in difficulties?'

'You could put it that way,' Kestrel returned scathingly. 'Why, is he to have the good fortune of being rescued by you?'

The bird's sarcasm was lost on Bold, who was more concerned with his family's whereabouts. 'Please tell me, Kestrel,' he begged, 'where he is – and the others, too.'

Kestrel relented a little as he recognized the real concern in the cub's voice. 'Your mother and sister are quite safe. They're lying low a little way ahead. Apparently your father went ahead on his own to the enemy camp, but your brother followed him.'

'You must get Vixen and Charmer back here with us straight away,' said Badger. 'Tell them Bold is safe. But surely, Scarface will have told Fox his cub is no longer with them?' he added on a thought.

'I don't know what they've told him, but Fox and Friendly are in real peril. They're completely surrounded by hostile animals.'

Bold gulped. 'I *must* help them. I caused the trouble,' he muttered woefully.

'You'll stay here with us,' Badger said sharply. 'When your mother and sister return, you must all go back to your den. Fox will find a way out of his predicament, I know.' But his words belied his true feelings, and he feared for his friend's safety.

Kestrel flew off again and soon Vixen and Charmer could be seen on the path back. Bold greeted them lavishly.

'I told Kestrel to pass on the news to Fox,' said Vixen. She looked at Badger worriedly. 'How will he ever get away?' she whispered.

'By superior cunning,' Mole answered confidently. 'Scarface is not in the same league.'

Vixen smiled thinly at Mole's attempt at cheerfulness. 'I believe he has Owl with him,' she said. 'Perhaps the two of them –' She broke off lamely. A miserable silence followed.

Bold became more and more restless. Then, suddenly, he cried out: 'Here's my brother coming!'

Friendly was indeed coming, but a more woeful, dejected beast would have been hard to find. He crept up to his mother and licked her muzzle forlornly. Then he looked at Bold. 'I'm glad to see you safe and unhurt,' he said. 'But we cubs and our mother are only allowed to be so at the expense of our father.'

All the animals began talking at once. 'What do you mean?' 'What's happened?' 'Is he dead?' 'What have they done to him?' came the cries.

Friendly looked at them all expressionlessly. 'So that I might go free, Fox has offered himself to the enemy to do with him what they will.'

'What *will* they do? Oh, this is too awful,' cried the anguished Vixen in despair. 'Friendly, you should have stayed with your father,' she moaned.

'I wanted to,' muttered her offspring, 'but he insisted – he ordered me away.'

'And Owl? Kestrel? Are they with him?' Vixen wailed.

'Oh yes,' he replied. 'The birds will stay with him. But what can they do amongst a dozen or so hostile foxes?'

'A dozen!' all the animals cried, looking from one to the other in horror, each one hoping another would make some sort of suggestion. Bold looked sicker and sicker with each passing minute. His sturdy form seemed to wilt as he felt the full impact of his recklessness.

Badger, as nominal leader, knew that it must be he who should make a decision. Yet what could he decide? The little band of friends was outnumbered and outmatched to a hopeless degree by a dozen foxes. He pondered miserably. The other animals found themselves, one by one, looking towards him for guidance.

Badger stood up and shook himself, trying to assume an expression of resolve. 'Well, my friends, we seem to be in a pretty pickle,' he said. 'We can't go forward and attack in the hope of freeing Fox, because we'd simply be hastening our own ends. Rabbits and squirrels and moles are not much of a test for an army of foxes. No, we can't risk anything like that. So I don't see any point in our remaining here; it would be far better to return to our homes while we can.'

The other animals looked at him in astonishment. 'We can't just abandon him, Badger,' said Weasel.

'No, no. *I* shall go to them. A supposed show of force would only antagonize. They must know me as a reasonable sort of fellow and I shall go along with the argument that they owe Fox something for his efforts last winter in ridding the Park of poachers.'

'That could be more of a hindrance than a help,' warned Weasel. 'Don't you remember how the poachers shot some foxes in the hope that one of them might be our Fox – because he caused so much annoyance? Scarface might argue that Fox had been responsible for these deaths rather than doing anyone a service.'

But Badger was not to be put off. 'At any rate,' he insisted, 'he *was* responsible for the capture of the poachers in the end by the Warden – and that was certainly a serviceable act for all the Park creatures. And, you see, I'm getting on in years now, and if anything should go wrong it's far better that it fall on my head rather than any of yours. You've got families or are still young and –'

'Oh, Badger!' cried Mole. 'Let me come! Don't go alone. Foxes won't bother with me. I'm of no account. I can't bear to think that anything might happen to you!'

Badger smiled at his adoring friend. 'No, Mole, old fellow, it wouldn't do. I'm very touched, but – well, I should be worrying about you all the time and that would be a bit of a hindrance, really, wouldn't it?'

Mole knew there was no answer to that argument.

'Now, everyone,' Badger went on. 'Please, all of you, go back home. Fox and I *will* come back all right – you'll see. Friendly, you'd better give me directions.'

This done, the brave old creature smiled shyly at them all and shambled away, leaving them to watch his disappearance almost before they had begun to accept it. It was in all their minds that, now both of their accepted leaders had placed themselves at risk, who in future would speak for the animals of Farthing Wood should anything untoward occur?

—8—

A Snake in the Grass

Such was Badger's faith in Fox's abilities that he became
more confident as he trotted along, thinking his
thoughts. He had no doubts that Fox could outwit his
opponent, given the opportunity. He also found it
difficult to imagine even the unpleasant Scarface exhorting
his clan to tear Fox to shreds in cold blood. His methods
were usually of a secretive nature – a surprise attack,
catching the victim unawares. He recalled how he himself
with Tawny Owl had thwarted Scarface at Fox's earth
when the cubs had been much younger, and so had
probably been blessed with his enmity ever since. But he
was not afraid. Like all the animals of Farthing Wood,
Badger was used to being on his guard – a habit induced
by the greater dangers that had prevailed in their old

home. So he was quite unprepared for the scene he found before him when he arrived at the spot.

Under a solitary Scots Pine, on which perched Tawny Owl and Kestrel, sat a very calm looking Fox. Facing him, and some yard or two away, stood Scarface and his assorted dependents. They were standing quite still. The space in the middle, between the two groups, was occupied by none other than the Great Stag, the leader of the White Deer herd which gave the Park its name. He seemed to be addressing all of them. No one noticed Badger coming along, so he too sat down a little way off, but near enough to hear what the Stag was saying . . .

'In my view all the inhabitants of the Reserve owe something to the animals who came here from Farthing Wood. The humans who came poaching last winter amongst my herd were a danger to all creatures, not just us deer, and it was due to Fox's bravery and resourcefulness, more than anything else, that the Park was finally rid of them.'

'Not without some loss of life to my clan,' Scarface growled.

'We too lost some of our numbers,' the Stag reminded him. 'And the toll could have been a lot higher on all sides had those men not been stopped.'

Scarface was silent. No animal cared to gainsay the inherent authority of the Great White Stag. The other foxes sat pensively, as if digesting the words they had heard. Badger wandered over to his friends by the pine tree.

'Er – I think now would be a good time to leave,' he whispered, and turned to give a greeting to the Stag. Fox nodded, and the two began to walk back along the path without exchanging further words. The two birds waited a little before they followed. The Stag seemed to feel the scene was at a close and made his exit.

Badger turned once as he and Fox proceeded quietly on their way. Scarface had remained motionless, an almost baffled expression on his face. He appeared to be conscious that somehow he had been outwitted, without quite realizing how this had been achieved. His dependents, to the last animal, watched him curiously as if waiting for a reaction. Meanwhile Badger and Fox were putting themselves at a safe distance.

'Well,' said Badger finally, 'the Great Stag's presence certainly saved the day. How did he come to be involved?'

'More by luck than judgement,' replied Fox. 'It was uncanny in a way. Quite suddenly he just materialized on the scene.'

'Did Kestrel fetch him perhaps?'

'No, no. The birds seemed as surprised as everyone else at his arrival.'

'There's more to this than meets the eye,' Badger rejoined, and fell to musing as they went along. No more was spoken on the subject for the time.

Their friends had all moved on from the earlier hiding-place and, as Fox was, naturally, still concerned for his family, Tawny Owl and Kestrel flew on to tell Vixen all were safe. Fox and Badger re-crossed the brook and, once on the other side, began to feel their relief. As they breasted their way through the long grass, a familiar figure reared up in their path. It was Adder.

There was something of a self-satisfied look in his expression that the preoccupied Fox did not at once notice. But Badger recognized it all right. 'Hallo,' he said knowingly. 'Do I detect the missing link in the recent chain of events?'

Fox looked a little puzzled as the snake's favourite leer was directed at Badger.

'How pleasant to see you both,' Adder hissed non-committally. 'This is developing into quite a parade. I've just watched the whole of the Farthing Wood community go past me.'

'Yes, indeed,' said Badger. 'And I know that the deer herd often go up to the stream there to drink. Perhaps you've seen *them* today too?'

'Aha!' cried Fox who had now got the thread of things. 'So you're the culprit, Adder!'

'Oh, I'm quite innocent in all respects,' Adder replied with feigned indifference. 'I often feel we snakes have a quite undeserved reputation for a sort of low cunning.'

'No, my friend, there is nothing low about you,' said Fox, 'apart, of course, from your necessary adaptation to life.'

Badger chuckled at the allusion, while Adder broadened his leer still further.

'Once again, I believe I am indebted to you,' Fox told him. 'But the result of my recent encounter will probably mean we shall all have to be even more cautious in the future.'

'I think one young creature has learnt his lesson today, at any rate,' Badger ventured to say.

'I'm sure he has,' Fox agreed. 'When I see him I shan't feel it necessary to raise the subject any further.'

Adder began to glide away.

'Before you go, Adder,' Fox called, 'where can we find you if we need you again?'

'I shall be within walking distance,' said the snake enigmatically. And Fox knew that that was the most he could get out of him.

'He saw the Stag all right,' Badger said as they continued on their way, 'and sent him in the general direction of the Scarface territory.'

'Yes,' said Fox. 'He'd hate to be counted reliable, but that's exactly what he is.'

From there it was not long before the two animals reached their homes. Badger went to his set, leaving Fox to be re-united with his family. A very humble Bold was the first to welcome him. Fox's only remark to him was: 'A little too much too soon, young fellow.'

—9—

A Wild Sort of Day

The following day the animals' attention was completely occupied by the weather. An immensely strong wind had got up and was bellowing through the Park, snapping saplings and bending grass into great rolling waves of threshing green. Even great trees were shaken where they stood; the newly leafed branches tossed and cracked in anguish, unloosing a furious shower of twigs on to the ground.

The smaller creatures cowered in their homes, shivering as they listened to the howls and screeches of the rushing air. Birds flew wildly from tree to swaying tree, unable to find a secure foothold. Only Kestrel stayed aloft, buffeted all round the sky like a ball of paper, and revelling in the wildness.

Unable to rest, Fox emerged from his den to investigate, leaving Vixen in charge. Every tuft of his fur was instantly assailed by the wind and blown all over the place. He narrowed his eyes against its fury and set off at a trot in no specific direction. In the woods he saw the trees heaving at their roots, like boats straining at anchor in a storm-tossed harbour. A creaking and moaning were audible everywhere. One small hawthorn tree cracked in two and crashed to earth, sending a frightened rabbit skipping away through the undergrowth. Rooks where wheeling over the tree-tops, raucously bemoaning their wrecked nests.

Fox saw a brownish shape spread wings and flit from one tree to another in a restless, disconcerted manner. He recognized Tawny Owl. He ran after him silently, knowing that if he called his words would be dashed to pieces by the strength of the wind. He caught up with Tawny Owl who looked down at him with an expression of alarm. 'This is terrible,' the bird cried. 'There's just no shelter anywhere.'

'You'd be better off on the ground,' Fox shouted back. 'It's firmer footing than any tree.'

Tawny Owl took his advice and then stood in a hunched attitude, looking slightly ridiculous with his feathers blown all awry. 'I hate this weather,' he complained. 'It's most undignified.'

'No good worrying about appearances,' Fox told him. 'You can't escape Nature.'

Tawny Owl snorted. He was not prepared to be consoled. They walked to a clearing in the trees and Owl pointed upwards with a jerk of his head.

'Look at that idiot Kestrel,' he grumbled. 'He's been up there all day.'

'He seems to be enjoying himself,' Fox commented.

'Precious little enjoyment in being blown to bits, I

should have thought,' replied Tawny Owl. 'Trust him to make a spectacle of himself.'

Fox chuckled at his friend's bad temper. 'Never mind,' he said. 'The wind's bound to blow itself out eventually.'

Just then an animal raced past them, out of the wood into the clearing, and dashed about in every conceivable direction in a completely aimless way. Fox and Tawny Owl looked at each other. 'Hare!' they both exclaimed together and laughed.

'He goes quite mad in this sort of weather,' said Tawny Owl. 'It's the same for all his kind.'

They watched Hare racing and leaping about, as if exhilarated by the day. Sometimes he would stop briefly and rear up on his hind legs, but a second later he would dash off again. Once he stood up and seemed to look right at them, but if he did he paid them no more attention than if they had been a couple of the dead leaves that were chasing each other over the ground.

'He wouldn't have noticed us if we had been directly in front of him,' Tawny Owl remarked. 'Every thought goes out of his head on such occasions.'

As Hare raced off again they were startled to see another animal running after him.

'It's a fox,' whispered Owl.

'And I know which one,' Fox answered grimly.

'Well, Hare's in no danger, anyway,' said Tawny Owl. 'There's no catching him.'

'Not if he runs in a straight line,' said Fox. 'But he's veering all over the place. In this mood, as you say, he's quite unaware of anything. He's just as capable of running himself into that creature's jaws as anything else.'

'Well, there's nothing we can do,' said Tawny Owl with a shrug, 'if he won't see or hear us.'

But Fox's fears proved to be groundless, for Hare had

evidently decided to finish capering for the time. He saw the alien fox as he stopped and lay down at a distance. Then he was up and bounding away at his matchless speed to complete safety.

Fox heaved a sigh of relief as Scarface, his enemy, consoled himself by lapping from a puddle in a hollow in the ground. His eyes looked straight ahead as he drank and, presently, he spotted his adversaries. With a muffled growl and a glare he slunk aside, eventually breaking into a slow trot.

'A nasty piece of animal flesh if ever I saw one,' remarked Tawny Owl. 'There'll be no hope of taking our ease as long as he's loose in the Park.'

'H'm. I'm afraid his occupation here is likely to be a lengthy one,' mused Fox. 'As he's told us, he'd been here a long time before we arrived. The Park is his home and must remain so, despite our wishes.'

'He must be of a great age?' wondered Owl.

'Who can say? But a hardier, tougher creature you'd find it difficult to meet. If there were any weakness in him from old age, he couldn't have survived that last terrible winter.'

'Pity!' ejaculated Tawny Owl. 'I know I'm pessimistic, but I've got the feeling that that character won't rest until he's done us some real harm.'

Fox looked at him sadly. 'You seem to forget, Owl,' he said quietly, without a hint of bitterness, 'that Scarface has already done that as far as Vixen and myself are concerned.'

'Oh! No, I . . .' stammered the bird, who *had* momentarily forgotten. 'I – I – didn't mean . . . I'm sorry, Fox,' he finished weakly.

'It's all right,' said his friend. 'Even we try not to think too much about her.'

The wind continued to howl horribly through the tree-tops. Weasel and Badger were the next to brave the elements, unable to rest. They came, complaining, up to the other two.

'I'm surprised you notice anything,' Tawny Owl said to Weasel. 'You're so slight and close to the ground.'

'Obviously, then, it hasn't occurred to you, that the frailer the body, the greater the damage,' Weasel answered sourly.

'Well, there *are* a lot of bad tempers being aired today,' said Fox.

'Wind creates bad temper,' said Weasel. 'A breeze is one thing, but this . . .'

He broke off as, just discernible through the wind's roar, the steady whistling beat of their friend the heron's wing could be detected. Presently his long body and thin trailing legs were seen approaching. He alighted and bowed to them in his old-world manner. 'A wild sort of day,' he commented.

'Very pleasant to see you about,' smiled Fox, as Whistler carefully arranged his one sound and one bullet-scarred wing across his back.

'I am glad to have seen you so soon,' the heron replied. 'I've been looking for you. I've just seen the scarred fox on the prowl and, from the look of him, he's up to no good.'

'He never is,' said Weasel. 'That's nothing new.'

'He was here,' Fox told them. 'Stalking Hare – quite uselessly, as it turned out. But thanks for coming anyway, Whistler.'

'He had an air about him,' said Whistler. 'An air of – er – how should I describe it? I think the word "wickedness" would suit as well as any other.'

'I believe you are right about that,' Tawny Owl agreed. 'That was the same sort of impression I got. It's as if he's determined to stir up trouble somehow.'

'Dear me. What can we do?' asked Badger.

'Nothing at all,' said Fox. 'He's free to roam where he will.'

'I hope the mice and voles are all under cover,' said Badger. 'They're so vulnerable.'

'At least Kestrel can keep a look-out while he's up there,' said Fox in rather a helpless sort of way.

'Humph! Not him!' grunted Tawny Owl disparagingly. 'He's too busy with his acrobatics to do anything useful. Such a show-off!'

'Now, Owl, I'm sure he plays his part as we all do,' Badger said. 'These are dangerous times and everyone is expected to use extra caution.'

'He never has a good word to say for Kestrel,' Weasel remarked bluntly. 'It's perfectly obvious there's a certain degree of jealousy in his attitude.'

'Jealousy! Jealousy?' expostulated Tawny Owl. 'And what is there to be jealous of in his tomfoolery? When Kestrel learns how to hunt in pitch blackness with pinpoint accuracy or to fly in total silence through the length of the Reserve without so much as a bat knowing about it, *then* I might have cause to envy him. But all he can do is to make an exhibition of himself.'

'Of course, you wouldn't concede there is a certain amount of skill or speed in *his* flying?' Weasel said sarcastically.

'That's enough, you two,' Fox said quietly. 'This is getting too ridiculous. If the wind puts you in this frame of mind, the best thing is to keep yourselves to yourselves.'

'Well, well,' intoned Whistler. 'And I've always looked upon you Farthing Wood creatures as inseparable. Perhaps a certain degree of tension in the air accounts for this contretemps?'

'I think there's a lot to be said for that observation,' said

Fox. 'Weasel, Owl, please – don't let's fall out amongst ourselves. There's never been a time when we should stick together more than now.'

'Yes, of course, Fox. I apologize,' said Weasel to Tawny Owl who looked away, ruffling his feathers.

'Owl?'

'Oh, very well. Er – sorry. To *Kestrel* I mean,' he said defiantly, glaring at Weasel.

The others laughed. Tawny Owl shuffled his feet, aware that he had ended up looking absurd again. But his discomfiture was soon forgotten. The unmistakable scream of a hare pierced even the deafening wind's bluster. The animals at once set off in a run towards the sound, while Tawny Owl and Whistler took to the air, the wind's fury forgotten.

Soon they saw Hare and his remaining leveret, now grown as big as himself, hurtling towards them. Their long elastic legs bounded over the ground.

'What is it?' Fox called. 'What's happened?'

Hare collapsed in a heap at his feet, great shuddering moans coming from him. He was unable to speak.

'It's my mother,' panted Leveret. 'Killed by Scarface.'

—10—
A Council of War

The animal's expressions on hearing the news showed a mixture of anguish and rage. But none of them appeared shocked. It was almost as if they had expected something of the kind to happen. Compassion for the two hares was their immediate concern, and they gave all the comfort they could which, for the most part, was unavailing.

Weasel was the first to voice all their thoughts. 'Now it's no longer just a quarrel between foxes,' he said. 'Whether we like it or not, we've all become implicated.'

Through his misery Hare said brokenly: 'This calls for revenge. She – she was slaughtered – just where she lay on her form. There was no warning. No scent, you see – the wind took that away . . .'

'Two deaths now in our community,' said Weasel, 'and the cause of both of them – Scarface.'

'We can't let this pass,' said Tawny Owl. 'We must fight back.'

'Oh dear,' said Badger worriedly. 'We mustn't do anything hastily. We have to be so careful. We're in the minority.'

'We will do nothing rash,' Fox said quietly. 'We shall plan properly. But Hare's mate didn't travel all that great distance from Farthing Wood to be savaged to death in her new home. If we have no security here we have nothing. This bloodthirsty creature doesn't kill for food but from envy and hatred of us.'

'I believe there is an element of fear in his behaviour,' observed Whistler.

'Yes,' agreed Fox. 'And he will have *reason* to fear us, too. I can promise him that.'

'Don't forget, Fox, our little band is weak compared with the forces Scarface can draw on,' warned Badger. 'We don't want to bite off more than we can chew. Wouldn't it, perhaps, be better to invoke the authority of the Great Stag in the affair?'

'Stuff and nonsense, Badger!' snorted Tawny Owl. 'What could he do? Scarface has just given the best possible demonstration of what he thinks of the Great Stag's authority!'

'Quite right, Owl,' said Fox. 'But there will be no pitched battle between the Farthing Wood animals and Scarface's army of foxes. Never fear, Badger,' he added reassuringly. 'It is subtlety that's called for here and that's where we have the advantage.'

No one paid any attention to the indirect compliment Fox paid himself, for they all knew he was the master of cunning. Only Tawny Owl liked to believe his own wits were a match for Fox's and he prepared himself to give the advice that would be needed.

But Fox continued: 'Scarface is our enemy. We have no real quarrel with his subordinates. I'm sure that they would do nothing on their own. That means we must eliminate their leader.'

'Do you mean *kill* him?' Leveret asked.

'Of course he does,' Tawny Owl chipped in. 'It's obvious that must be our first move.'

'Not first move, Owl. *Only* move,' said Fox calmly.

'Oh – um – yes, naturally. Er – would that be sufficient, do you think?' Tawny Owl answered, trying hard to appear full of wisdom.

'I think so,' replied Fox. 'Scarface is the trouble-maker. Without his presence, I am convinced the other foxes wouldn't interfere any further with us. So we have to find a way of removing that presence.'

'If I thought I could achieve that,' said Hare, 'I'd willingly sacrifice myself.'

'No!' said Fox shortly. 'My dear friend, we want no more sacrifices. I don't want another life lost.'

'No, no,' said Tawny Owl importantly. 'No *one* of us is equal to a contest. But together . . .'

'Together, what?' queried Weasel mischievously, who was quite aware of Tawny Owl's high opinion of himself.

'Quite clearly we have to ambush him,' came the peremptory answer.

'What, all of us?'

'Certainly.'

'Including the voles and fieldmice? Yes, I'm sure they would be very useful, Tawny Owl.'

'Er – humph! Well, no, not them specifically. You know I didn't mean *literally* – er – well, the whole – er – of us,' the bird spluttered.

Fox came to his rescue. 'I think I have a better plan,' he announced, 'though ambush does come into it, in a way.'

Tawny Owl completely regained his self-composure at these words and stretched his wings in a haughty way while he directed a look at Weasel which quite plainly said: 'You see!'

'I'm thinking along the lines of a great deal of stealth and surprise being used,' explained Fox. 'That would certainly be necessary. Now, who do you think fits best into that category?'

'Are you perhaps referring to yourself?' queried Badger.

'No, not at all,' answered Fox. 'I'm far too big. As I see it, there is only one candidate. He is capable of lying in Scarface's path, completely hidden. And he has the capacity to kill with one blow.'

'You can only be thinking of Adder?' remarked Whistler.

'Exactly,' said Fox. 'Scarface would be poisoned. Now, the only difficulty I can foresee is Adder himself. Will he cooperate?'

'Well, Fox, you know, he's such a strange creature,' said Badger. 'There's no knowing how he would react to such a suggestion.'

'Surely there *is* only one way to react?' said Hare. 'Is he with us or not?'

'That is never in doubt,' Fox said stoutly. 'But he does hate being told what to do. If we could somehow put it in his mind that he is the key to our safety, there would be no question of his not acting. He would make the decision himself and woe betide us if we should praise him afterwards.'

'That's Adder all over,' admitted Weasel. 'Well then, someone has to have a little talk with him.'

'Who is closest to him?' queried Hare.

'No one's close to Adder,' remarked Tawny Owl.

'Well, who is he most receptive to?'

'How about Toad?' suggested Weasel.

'That might work,' agreed Fox. 'But Toad would have to be found first and I don't know anyone who's seen him recently.'

'Toad's not the one for this job,' said Tawny Owl deprecatingly. 'It calls for someone with the utmost subtlety.'

'That lets you out then,' said Weasel rudely, who saw where Tawny Owl's remark was supposed to lead.

'How dare you!' he snapped. 'We all know *you're* incapable anyway.'

'Now, now,' Fox pleaded. 'Don't start again. D'you know, I think innocence may serve as well as guile with Adder? Then he's less likely to suspect he's being used.

'Now my cub, Bold, is always talking of the snake. I think he really admires him, and Adder probably knows it. He might be just what we're looking for.'

'An excellent idea, Fox,' enthused Badger. 'And Bold will feel he is going some way towards making up for his recent misdemeanour.'

'Then it's settled,' said Fox. 'I shall go and speak to him straight away. He can search out Adder tomorrow and the thing will be done.'

'Will you let us know how things go?' Weasel wanted to know.

'Yes. Let's meet again and Bold himself can tell you,' suggested Fox. 'In the meantime, Hare, you and Leveret must lie low. Farewell to you all for the moment.'

'Is Adder's venom really so powerful?' Leveret asked as Fox trotted away.

'I believe so,' Badger answered him. 'I understand even humans are fearful of snakebite.'

'Then he carries a deadly weapon indeed,' the young hare murmured. 'How I wish he had been close at hand when my mother was attacked.'

—11—
Bold and Cunning

Bold, of course, received his father's suggestion enthusi-astically. He was overjoyed to be chosen to undertake the important mission of priming Adder. His brother, Friendly, was also keen to be involved and pestered his father to let him go too, until he eventually relented.

'Very well,' said Fox. 'I suppose there's no harm in it, as long as you leave Bold to do most of the talking.'

This confidence in his ability made Bold positively glow but, far from becoming conceited, he was only too aware of the trust being put in him. Fox explained to him Adder's whereabouts.

'We'll leave early,' said Bold. 'There's no time to be lost where lives are at stake.'

So, just after first light on the next day, he and Friendly

left the den to search for the unsuspecting Adder. Fox turned to Vixen and said: 'If he's successful in this, I think he's entitled to a little more independence. If he shows signs of wanting to leave the earth permanently, we must let him.'

'I never expected to have to chase *him* away from the family home,' remarked Vixen, 'but it's a task that often falls to the mother fox when the cubs are too clinging.'

'Yes, that's certainly one of the less pleasant of a vixen's duties,' remarked her mate. 'In your case, it may be our other two cubs who have to be chivvied a little.'

Vixen said: 'I think Friendly will go wherever his brother goes. It's this one who could be the problem.' She nodded towards Charmer who was still sleeping.

'Unless, of course, she should find herself a mate,' Fox pointed out.

Bold and Friendly went cautiously in the direction of the long grass and bracken that was close to the boundary stream. This was certainly where they expected to find Adder. After the previous day's rumbustiousness, this morning was calm, fresh and full of scents.

'What a wonderful morning to be out adventuring!' Friendly exclaimed to his larger brother cub.

'It's a very serious undertaking we're entrusted with,' said Bold. 'We should feel honoured.'

Friendly looked thoughtful. 'I hope we don't let anyone down,' he said doubtfully. 'Supposing we can't find Adder?'

'If Adder's around, he'll be sure to be keeping an eye open on everyone's comings and goings,' Bold replied confidently.

'Mole says his eyes are always open,' chirped Friendly as they entered the long grass, 'because snakes don't have eyelids.'

'Nonsense,' said Bold. 'How does he sleep then?'

'Perhaps Adder doesn't need to,' answered Friendly. 'He's not very active.'

Bold paused to scratch his flank. 'If you think that, you can certainly never have seen him stalking his prey. When he strikes, he's like lightning.'

'Thanks for the compliment, youngster,' came a drawling voice close at hand. Presently Adder slithered into view. 'It's a rarity to hear anyone saying anything pleasant about me.'

Bold felt he had made a splendid start. 'I know my father and mother have nothing but good to say of you,' he added eagerly.

Adder chuckled drily. 'That's loyalty for you,' he lisped.

Bold was not sure if he was referring to himself or his parents. Adder was looking at him penetratingly. 'Were you searching for me by any chance?' he asked.

'Oh no,' Bold fibbed. 'We were – er – just enjoying an outing.'

'Yes, that's it. Just adventuring,' Friendly chipped in.

Adder held Bold's gaze for a moment longer. 'Well,' he said at length, 'I'm glad to have seen you.' He seemed to be about to move on.

'Er – won't you stay a little longer, Adder?' Bold asked hurriedly. 'We – we don't see you often.'

Adder's expression remained inscrutable, but a glint came into his red eyes. He was beginning to see how the land lay. 'All right,' he responded. 'Delighted to be in such demand, I'm sure.' The sardonic tone to his voice was now unmistakable. Friendly began to look flustered but Bold struggled to appear cool. He tried to think of an opening to the all-important subject. Adder waited.

'My – er – my parents send their regards,' he said.

'Thank you. Did they expect you to see me then?'

'Well, no. But, you see, they knew we might come this way and, of course, well – you're often about,' Bold floundered, looking round at Friendly for support.

'Ah yes, I did say I would be hereabouts,' Adder said knowingly. 'Are Fox and Vixen well?'

'Oh yes. *They* are,' replied Bold with evident relief at the looked-for opportunity presenting itself.

'You imply that someone is not well?' Adder rejoined.

'Hare's mate was killed,' Friendly announced rather baldly.

'That is bad news,' said Adder. 'How did it happen?'

'She was killed by Scarface,' Bold answered.

Adder's intuition had by now grasped the true purport of the cubs' appearance. Their inexperience was no match for his slyness. He knew they had been sent to look for him for some purpose. He laid a trap for them.

'No doubt Fox wants all the Farthing Wood band to avenge in some way this latest death?'

Friendly fell straight into the trap. 'No, not all. Just one,' he blurted out. Bold glared at him.

'I see, I see,' Adder hissed. 'And where do I fit in?' (He knew perfectly well, of course.)

'My father merely wanted you to know what had occurred,' Bold said, hoping to retrieve the situation, 'so that, if you felt you could help in any way, er – well –'

'I would do so?' leered the snake. 'Yes, yes, you need say no more. I understand perfectly.' He was enjoying himself. 'I'm to be the tool to carry out the job.'

'Why didn't you keep quiet?' Bold snapped angrily at his brother. 'You heard my father. It was to be left to *me*.'

'Oh dear, oh dear,' sighed Adder. 'Do I detect a slight lack of rapport?'

'I should have come alone,' muttered Bold.

Adder was greatly amused by the young foxes'

discomfiture. In his smoothest manner he said: 'You really don't have to find an excuse to visit me, you know I shall always be pleased to see you. I have thoroughly enjoyed our little chat.'

Bold's pride in his selection by his father was now utterly deflated. He had simply not been clever enough for the likes of Adder. His crestfallen appearance, however, stirred a flicker even in the snake's dry old heart.

'You may tell your father that I shall do all in my power to even the score,' he told the cub, 'and,' he added, 'nothing would give me greater pleasure.'

Bold pricked up his ears and looked at Adder in astonishment.

'Next time you come to see me,' said that knowing reptile, 'I hope it will be solely for our mutual pleasure.'

Then he was off, weaving his patterns through the long stalks of grass and producing only the barest rustle of noise.

'I believe even our father could be outwitted by his cunning,' Bold whispered in admiration, and wondered if he heard an answering chuckle through the fern fronds.

'We did it! We did it!' crowed Friendly.

But Bold was too happy to reprimand him again and turned hastily back to tell Fox of the result of their encounter. 'Listen, Friendly,' he said. 'There's no need for us to mention that Adder guessed we had been sent deliberately. After all, our triumph will be marred a little if we admit we were bested.'

'Isn't that being dishonest?' Friendly asked innocently.

'Even if it is, it doesn't matter. We've achieved the required result, haven't we? Scarface will be killed, and that's all that matters.'

Friendly was not happy about hiding the complete

truth, but decided he would say no more as he had already come close to wrecking the whole plan. Yet Bold's lack of honesty was to prove a costly mistake, and one which he was to regret for a very long time.

—12—
Death of a Fox

Fox and Vixen were proud and delighted at the outcome of their cubs' meeting with Adder, and Fox lost no time in spreading the good news that the snake was ready and willing to strike against Scarface. The other animals were relieved and, some, a little surprised that the immature Bold had succeeded so easily in implanting the idea in Adder's subtle brain.

Tawny Owl had said: 'So he fell for it, did he? All credit to the youngsters, then. It's no easy matter to hoodwink that rascal.'

Hare was particularly satisfied. 'I'm only impatient for the thing to take place,' he told Fox. 'It'll bring a measure of security to creatures like the rabbits and ourselves who feel specially at risk.'

Badger was the last to hear and, despite sharing all the creatures' relief, was still a little doubtful as to what might follow. 'I only hope you're right about the other foxes' lack of aggression,' he remarked to his friend. 'If they should decide to gang up on us afterwards, there's no knowing how many deaths could occur.'

'Don't worry,' said Fox calmly. 'They will have no leader. With Scarface out of the way they will have no one to motivate them. He brooks no rivals in his neck of the woods, so it's certain that he won't have groomed a successor.'

'When does Adder expect to do it?'

'Who can say, Badger? He must wait for the right opportunity.'

'And then – when it's done – how long before we know?' Badger persisted.

'Only so long as it takes Adder to find one of us,' said Fox. 'Unless, of course, Kestrel spots anything. I know he means to keep a sharp look-out for Scarface's movements.'

'Oh dear, I wish it were all over,' Badger sighed. 'Our lives have been fraught with anxiety recently. It'll be a welcome change to be able to wander about freely again without feeling the need to keep turning one's head.'

But things turned out to be not at all as anyone had expected. Some days passed before they were all to learn the true situation that had arisen. The chain of events that led to the discovery of the truth began with Whistler deciding to fish further upstream than he usually did.

He and his mate had been standing patiently in the shallows of the boundary stream, watching for a likely catch. From the corner of his eye Whistler detected a moving shape on the bank. He looked up. It was a young fox he had not seen before who was tracking the water-rats. Although he had crossed to the 'wrong' side of the stream his pursuit appeared harmless enough (except to the water-rats) and Whistler went back to peering into the water. He became thoroughly absorbed again, and he and his mate were eventually able to make a hearty meal. When they were quite satisfied, Whistler looked around again for a sign of the stranger. He spied him a long way off, still wandering along quite innocently. The heron was surprised to see the animal jerk suddenly to one side and utter a sharp yap of alarm. He watched a little longer, but as nothing further developed, he forgot the incident and, tucking one leg up comfortably, prepared to join his mate for a nap.

They awoke as the sun was sinking. A series of piteous howls, each more protracted than the last, sounded close by. For a while Whistler had difficulty in locating the noise, but finally traced it to the same fox he had seen earlier.

'Is he in pain?' his mate enquired.

'It sounds distinctly like it,' agreed Whistler. 'I think I'll investigate.'

He found the fox staggering heavily in an uncertain way in no particular direction. His breath was coming in gasps and, even as the heron watched, his legs seemed to give way and he fell on his side. He made efforts to get up again, but his limbs only trembled spasmodically, appearing to be all but paralysed. Whistler at once divined the cause. Adder had bitten the wrong animal.

There was no saving the creature now. His end was near. For a moment Whistler wondered what to do first and, even as he hesitated, other foxes loomed out of the dusk on the other side of the stream, attracted by the dying animal's cries. They called to him and he replied weakly. Now Whistler was awake to the danger at hand.

He was not afraid for Adder, who would obviously have made good his escape long before. But if the fox was able to identify the particular snake that had attacked him, the information would soon be passed to his kind. Scarface would not take the action lying down. Whistler knew his duty. He swiftly flew back to his mate.

'Something has gone horribly wrong,' he told her. 'Adder has made a terrible mistake. We must warn our friends that Scarface is still alive, and the wrong fox has been killed. Find all of them you can and pass the word. I will go this way. We must be quick. Goodness knows what may happen now if Scarface suspects the worst.'

As the two herons set off in urgent search of the Farthing Wood creatures, Scarface himself arrived on the scene as the poisoned fox died. The others who had crossed the stream suspected nothing of the significance of the death. Their relative had disturbed a snake and paid the penalty for alarming it. But the hardened veteran of their tribe had a different nature. He sniffed the dead animal carefully for any clue. Then he sat down and stared at his minions.

'An unusual occurrence,' he remarked to them; but none responded. He looked from one to the other. 'You had, each of you, better go more carefully in future. Snakes should be avoided unless you're sure you can handle them. I myself have killed a good number in my time. Yes, and eaten them. Have any of you seen the snake in question?'

They shook their heads.

'There is one snake who is often to be seen in this area,' said the wily Scarface. 'If any of you should happen to see it around, perhaps you will let me know.' Then he turned his back on them and swam back across the stream.

Whistler flew straight to Fox and called him out of his earth. Fox looked grim when he had heard all. 'What on earth is Adder up to?' he demanded. 'This is no time for playing pranks. Now we're all in trouble.'

'Could he have mistaken the other animal for

Scarface?' asked Whistler.

'Not Adder,' Fox replied firmly. 'Scarface is unmistakable. I shall have a few sharp words to say to our friend when he comes to report his deed. In the meantime we shall have to post sentries in case of an attack. You go on, Whistler, and warn the rabbits and the hares to keep well out of sight.'

Fox ran off to round up Badger, Weasel and Tawny Owl. Then he positioned them and himself and Vixen at different look-out points where they remained through the dark hours. At dawn, after a quiet night, they disbanded and Fox lay above ground to await Adder. Kestrel, high up above alien territory guarded all of them.

The morning wore on. Inside Fox's earth Bold dreaded the appearance of Adder. If the snake were accused of inviting new danger he would have no qualms in placing the blame fairly and squarely on the shoulders of the cub. Vixen noticed his nervousness, while Friendly's distress was even more apparent. However, she wisely held her tongue until the cubs revealed themselves.

Early in the afternoon Adder approached Fox's den. He saw Fox drowsing, head on paws in the warm sun, and calmly coiled himself up until Fox should wake. When he did so, Adder was wearing a distinctly smug and self-satisfied expression.

'I don't know what you're looking so pleased about,' Fox growled. 'We've heard of your achievement from Whistler. If I may say so, I think you behaved in the most irresponsible manner.'

Adder's expression froze and, as always, he betrayed not an inkling of his feeling. 'You may say exactly as you please,' he hissed quietly, 'for all the effect it will have on me.'

Fox glared at him. 'Really, Adder, I've always credited

you with more sense. As if the situation hadn't been bad enough already . . .'

'Er – what situation are you referring to?' Adder asked coolly.

'Oh, stop playing games!' spluttered Fox angrily. 'I'm talking of the animosity between us and Scarface's brood.'

'It seems as if I took my life in my hands for no purpose,' Adder observed. 'Having redressed the balance of our most recent loss, I now find I was not expected to do anything of the kind.'

Fox relented a little as he recognized reluctantly that Adder must have put himself at some considerable risk for the enterprise. 'But Adder,' he reasoned, 'why act so rashly? If it had meant waiting a few days more for the correct target to show, what would it have mattered?'

'Target?' queried Adder. 'I don't follow you.'

'Do you mean to tell me that you didn't know the target was Scarface?'

'Ah, I begin to understand your reaction,' said Adder. 'I'm afraid I have to disillusion you. No mention was made of Scarface to me by either of your – er – messengers.'

'W H A T?' exploded Fox so loudly that Bold heard him inside the earth.

'It was merely put to me that I was to avenge the death of Hare's mate – which I have done,' the snake explained. 'I'm afraid the significance of killing Scarface himself didn't occur to me.'

'It was the whole point of the thing,' Fox said wearily. 'We decided that, as he is the only real threat to our safety, he should be put out of the way. I was quite sure in my mind that none of his band would have had the idea of blaming his death on us. But it appears we have all been labouring under a misapprehension.'

'I'm afraid we have,' agreed Adder. 'Perhaps you should have questioned your offspring more closely?'

'I'll question him now,' said Fox meaningfully. 'Bold! Come out here!' he bellowed down.

The cub emerged sheepishly from the earth. 'It's all my fault, Father,' he said in a low voice. 'Adder told us that he would even the score, and I assumed he would attack Scarface.'

'How could you assume such a thing when you never even mentioned Scarface's name?' Fox demanded. 'Now see what has happened. You've succeeded in creating a more dangerous situation than before by your dishonesty. You failed in the task I gave you but reported it as a success.'

Bold hung his head and Adder felt disposed to put in a good word. 'I suppose I'm partly to blame,' he said generously. 'I should have realized where your thinking lay. However, the prospect may not be quite as perilous as you imagine. I'm quite sure I wasn't recognized by my victim, and there are many other adders in the Park.'

'A small grain of comfort, I'm afraid, Adder,' said Fox, shaking his head. 'I know Scarface. He won't rest until he's proved his own suspicions and then – woe betide us all.'

—13—
A Matter of Heart

Fox and Adder parted, each with a certain amount of self-reproach. The snake was privately furious with himself for not recognizing where the main danger to his friends lay, and he decided at once to make good what he should have done before. But this he kept to himself. As for Fox, although he ticked off Friendly for being an accomplice of Bold's dishonesty, he then let the matter drop. He felt a share of guilt himself for placing too much confidence in his inexperienced cubs.

While the animals took turns to keep watch at night for the dreaded coming of Scarface, Adder lay low and pondered how he could get at him now that the beast would be more wary than ever.

Scarface, of course, had his spies and soon discovered

that the Farthing Wood creatures were on guard at night. This served to confirm his earlier suspicions that the killing of his dependent had been no accident. He resolved to first settle the score with Adder, and then attack the rest of the community in the daytime, catching Adder's friends unawares.

However, it was no easy matter tracking a snake who knew he was in danger. Adder, like all his kind, spent most of his life among the roots of bracken and heather and was not often encountered in the open. Sometimes hot sunshine would tempt him out to bask, but Scarface was not foolish enough to expect Adder to go in for any sunbathing at present. If any snake *was* seen to be basking now, it would not be the one he was after. Thus Scarface and Adder were now committed enemies. So cautious did they become that they both might have been rendered invisible. It remained to be seen who should be the first to break cover.

This situation gave a breathing space to Fox and his friends. The nights were unusually quiet and uneventful and Fox considered relaxing the guard duty he had imposed. But Vixen warned him against it.

'That might be just what Scarface is waiting for,' she said. 'He's very clever and could be trying to wear us down.'

'Yes.' Fox sighed. 'You're probably right – as usual. Your advice is sound and I'll abide by it.'

'There's something uncanny about the quietness at night,' Vixen remarked. 'It's unnatural.'

'It can stay as quiet as this for ever for my liking,' Fox replied. 'At least no more lives will be lost.'

Vixen nodded. 'I think you could give the cubs a turn of guard duty,' she said. 'The training will be useful and it'll take some of the weight off the rest of us.'

Fox agreed and Bold, Friendly and Charmer were

thrilled to be of use. Bold, in particular, was grateful to be given another chance after his previous failure.

One night while he was keeping watch, Friendly and Charmer went their separate ways to hunt. They were allowed to do this as long as they did not stray too far. Friendly kept religiously close to home in his wanderings, but Charmer was rather less careful, and realized suddenly she was a long way from the den. She had caught nothing and was loth to return with an empty stomach. She gave herself a few moments longer before she must make her way back. As she trotted along, muzzle to the ground, searching for a scent, she became aware that she was being watched. She paused, one front paw raised, to sniff the air. The unmistakable scent of fox was in the air. Her body went rigid as she looked about her. She saw a pair of eyes glinting in the bright moonlight. A figure approached.

'I've seen you before,' it said. Charmer was relieved to see it was just a cub like herself.

'Yes, I recognize you,' she responded. 'You are one of Scarface's cubs.'

'I'm Ranger,' he told her. 'Once I met your brother: the big cub.'

'That's Bold,' she said. 'I am called Charmer.'

'I can well understand why,' Ranger told her gallantly.

Charmer looked taken aback. 'I – I must return home,' she muttered.

'Not on my account,' said Ranger. 'I bear you no ill will. This quarrel is none of my doing. It is our parents' battle.'

'My sister cub was killed by your father,' said Charmer sullenly. 'We have no love for your tribe.'

'I understand,' answered Ranger. 'But I am not responsible for my father's actions. He is a jealous animal and a proud one. I am only a fox cub.'

Charmer looked steadily at him. He was talking sense. 'For my part, I think it's regrettable we can't all live in peace,' she said.

'I'm of the same opinion,' Ranger agreed. 'Perhaps our generation see it differently.'

Charmer sighed. 'Nevertheless our loyalty lies with our family,' she reminded him.

'That is true,' Ranger said flatly.

There was a pause. 'Er – are you hunting?' he asked her.

Charmer smiled. 'Unsuccessfully,' she answered.

'If you're hungry, I can show you good sport,' Ranger offered. 'There's a colony of mice nearby.'

Charmer hesitated. She wondered if any of them were the fieldmice she was forbidden to kill – the old companions of her father.

'Do come,' the young fox urged her softly. 'It's much more fun hunting with another.'

Charmer relented and followed where he led to a patch of scrub. 'There's a regular nest of them in there,' he said. Satisfied that the spot was too far away from the home area for any Farthing Wood mice to be involved, Charmer's mouth began to water in anticipation.

Ranger looked at her and said: 'I'll see if I can drive them out to you.' And he did just that. In no time Charmer had pounced on four plump creatures and had made short work of them. She was appreciative of Ranger's interest.

'You're very skilful in coaxing them into the open,' she smiled.

'Ah. I'm getting quite familiar with the ways of these mice,' he said, smiling back. 'I often spend an odd hour here. Sometimes I just stalk them if I'm not hungry.'

'I'm surprised there are any left,' Charmer laughed.

They looked at each other for a long moment and

something indefinable passed between them. Charmer looked away shyly. 'Thank you for taking the edge off my appetite,' she said softly. 'But I must be going. My brothers may come looking for me.'

'I'll come some of the way with you,' Ranger said hopefully.

'No.' She answered quickly, thinking of Bold's reaction if he should see them together.

'As you wish,' he said in a regretful tone.

'I'm sorry,' Charmer said quietly. 'I think it's best.'

'Well, I hope we may meet on another occasion,' Ranger said, leaving a question in the air. 'As I said, I often come to this spot. You will know the way now, I think.'

'Yes, but I don't always come as far as this,' she replied non-committally. But, even as she said it, she knew she would return.

'A safe journey back,' Ranger wished her.

'Thank you. The same to you.' Charmer smiled sweetly and set off at a trot for home. Ranger watched her go. His blood was singing in his veins. The thought of his father and of the young she-cub's parent was a long way from his mind.

Charmer saw Friendly ahead as she approached the earth.

'I was out looking for you,' said her brother. 'Were you lucky in your hunting?'

'Yes, very lucky,' Charmer answered rather breathlessly.

Friendly looked at her sharply. She seemed to be glowing with health, and there was something in her tone – he was not quite sure what. He questioned her no further and said nothing as they passed the spot where Bold was lying hidden. But he decided he would stay closer to his sister on their next outing.

*

The next night was Friendly's watch and Bold showed no sign of wanting to keep Charmer company. He preferred to be alone. Charmer went straight to the patch of scrub but Ranger was not there. She was bitterly disappointed. She waited a little, passing the time by pouncing on unsuspecting mice. Of course, it was not likely (she told herself) that he would come to that place every night. But she kept her ears cocked to catch every faint sound. At last, when she had given up all hope, she heard the sound of approaching feet and her every nerve tensed. She knew it was Ranger for she recognized his scent. He came carefully, snuffling the air for any strange smell. Then he saw her. They smiled at each other.

'I'm very glad to see you,' he said, wagging his tail.

'Oh, I – I felt like mousehunting,' she whispered. He caught her expression and they both laughed.

'I've caught some water-rats,' he said. 'Will you share them with me?'

'Where are they?'

'Oh, not far. Up by the stream.'

'Oh, no, I couldn't, I'm afraid,' Charmer said. 'It's too far for me. I'm not supposed to wander that far afield.'

'Oh, I see. Well, perhaps I could bring them a little nearer,' he suggested.

'That would be very kind,' she murmured.

Ranger loped off and soon returned carrying two carcasses. 'You start on those,' he said generously, 'and I'll fetch the rest.'

A few minutes later they were enjoying their meal together.

'It's amazing how famished I get,' said Ranger between mouthfuls. 'Soon I hope to hunt for bigger game.'

Charmer thought of Hare's mate and let the comment pass unanswered.

'You have a good appetite yourself,' Ranger went on approvingly, and Charmer knew what he was leading up to.

'I don't know if it would be possible for us to hunt together,' she told him. 'We might run into my brothers, or, worse still, my father.'

'Would that matter?' Ranger asked innocently. 'We mean no harm.'

'I don't think my family would see it that way,' she replied softly.

The words were hardly out of her mouth when Ranger froze and pricked up his ears. There was an angry growling close by and then Bold raced on to the scene, hackles rising. Charmer had not reckoned with his more venturesome spirit. Luckily she was obscured by a low branch of the shrubs and only Ranger had been seen. She decided the best course of discretion was to make herself scarce. Ranger stood his ground, though nervously.

Bold stopped dead, his fangs bared and his tail swishing incessantly like an aggressive cat's. He had no intention of attacking the smaller cub, but had hoped to frighten it away and achieve a moral victory for himself. But Ranger met his fierce gaze steadily.

'You're a cool customer,' Bold acknowledged, despite himself. 'You seem to have gained a little in stature since we last encountered one another.'

'I have a new source of confidence,' Ranger answered him enigmatically.

'Well, I have no wish to fight you now,' said Bold. 'The Park is as much yours as mine.'

'I'm not looking for any trouble,' said Ranger. 'Why need we assume we're on opposing sides?'

Bold laughed shortly. 'I think your father can be left to explain that to you,' he commented. 'I'm sure that one day he will see to it that you and I join battle.' Then he left the other fox standing where he was. No trace of Charmer was to be seen.

On his way back to the family den, Bold paused for a word with Friendly. 'Have you seen our sister?' he asked. 'There's a strange fox-cub abroad and she should keep out of harm's way.'

'Oh yes, I've seen her,' replied Friendly with the ghost of a smile, at once understanding the situation. 'And I can assure you,' he added pointedly, 'I've never seen her looking better.'

Bold had no reason to read anything into his words, and thought no more of the matter apart from reporting his meeting to his father. As for Friendly – he liked to think the best of everyone, as his name implied, and he certainly was not going to expose any secrets his sister might have. He only stuck to his decision to see for himself, when the occasion should arise, how serious the affair was becoming.

—14—
Adder at Bay

For days Adder remained in hiding, confining himself to a small area of dense vegetation not far from the boundary stream. He was completely concealed but could detect any movement by others close by. In this way he hoped to catch Scarface off guard when the fox decided to begin his wanderings again. Also Adder was deliberately starving himself. He wanted to maintain his store of venom intact – there was none to spare on his usual prey.

Going without food was no problem for Adder. As a reptile a good meal could last him many days, provided he did not move around much and use up too much energy. In his present, rather torpid, state he could fast for a long while. It was not until about the seventh day that the first pangs of hunger struck him, and even then they were mild enough to be ignored. However, Adder was experiencing another sort of problem. He was cold. A spell of very cool, cloudy weather had prevailed for a time and, in his dark place of concealment, no spark of sunlight filtered through to warm his blood. Unlike his mammal friends, the snake could not regulate his body temperature internally – that was why in the cold winter months he was obliged to hibernate. He relied entirely on external warmth to keep himself active, and he knew that if he could not heat his blood sufficiently first, he would be simply too sluggish to move against the enemy with the necessary speed when conditions permitted.

More days passed and Adder became more and more torpid. Then one morning he knew the sun was beaming again. He was desperate for warmth and knew that, come what may, he must venture forth and bask for a spell if his plan was to go forward. With the utmost care, he slid slowly from his screen of vegetation and found a small open space surrounded by bracken where the sun could be enjoyed in seclusion. There had been neither sign nor sound of Scarface and his tribe. But, unfortunately for Adder, he had no idea that Ranger was making nightly trips across the stream to keep tryst with his new friend and that, on this particular morning, he was returning late to his father's territory.

The cub, after his latest meeting with Charmer, had been so full of spirits that he had run the length and breadth of the Reserve in his new mood of confidence. The dawn had begun to break as he had lain, intently watching the activity of a ginger cat inside the perimeter of the Warden's garden. It was an animal he had not come across before, and it was only the eventual disappearance of the cat that had set him in motion again on his homeward trail. As luck would have it, as he approached the banks of the stream again, he had chased a rabbit into the very clump of bracken that fringed the sunbathing Adder. Ranger saw the snake and immediately recalled his father's words. He ran straight off to tell him.

Scarface received the news without enthusiasm. 'A snake is a snake,' he said. 'But I doubt if it is the one *I'm* interested in. He is far too secretive.'

'Well, he's lying not far from the spot where our cousin was killed,' Ranger persisted. 'Shall we investigate?'

'I think not,' Scarface replied sourly. 'You look in need of a rest.'

'Oh no, Father, I feel quite fresh,' Ranger asserted.

'That's for me to decide,' Scarface remarked bluntly, and the cub knew he was dismissed.

The old fox sat alone and contemplated. Although it was unlikely that the basking snake was the one he wanted, he could not afford to ignore even a slender chance. There might be some way of trapping the creature into admitting its guilt. If it appeared unsuspicious of him – well, he could still kill it anyway. One poisonous snake less was no bad thing. But he wanted no companions. This exercise called for all his timeless skill and cunning. He trotted in a half circle from his den and crossed the brook downstream. Then he slunk noiselessly and slowly towards the patch of bracken Ranger had described. His paws made no sound on the ground.

Under and through the stalks of fern went Scarface. His feet trod carefully on the soft ground, but even he was unable to avoid just the barest rustle as he brushed the dry fern fronds of last year. Adder detected nothing until the fox, in a final burst, breasted through the last clump to the clearing.

The snake wriggled quickly to one side as Scarface leapt out at him, his teeth showing. Then a chase began as Adder bolted for thicker cover, while his pursuer jumped

this way and that, trying to head him off. Escape was now
the only thing in Adder's mind – a counterattack was
impossible. The element of surprise, essential when
attacking a larger animal, was lost in this instance.
Scarface snapped again and again, but amongst the
bracken Adder was difficult quarry. The fox snarled with
frustration. 'You – can't – get away,' he panted. 'You must
pay – the – penalty – for daring – to attack – one of my –
tribe.'

Adder was too busy to answer, even had he the
inclination. So Scarface still had no idea if he were
pursing the right snake. At last, just as Adder appeared to
be cornered and the fox made a lunge, the snake found a
hole in the ground and shot into it. But he was not quick
enough. Scarface's ancient teeth closed on the end of his
tail and held him fast. An agonizing tug of war followed.
Adder grimly tried to pull himself away while Scarface's
grip tightened as he attempted to haul the snake clear of
the hole. During the struggle Adder's tail was actually
bitten right through and the surprised fox was left
holding over an inch of his vanished quarry in his jaws.

Deep in the burrow, Adder nursed his wound. It was a
severe one but not fatal. When the pain subsided a little
he took stock of his position. He knew Scarface would
now wait outside the hole, hoping for his reappearance.
How long he would wait Adder could not guess. But he
could outlast the fox's appetite; of that he was quite sure.
Now he thought of the trouble brought on himself by his
attempt to help his friends, and he felt very aggrieved.
Why had he involved himself in a dispute between foxes
or, at best, between mammals? He would have done
better to leave them to their own dirty work. If he
survived his injury, his body would remain mutilated for
all time. He thought bitter thoughts. After a time he
painfully turned himself round in the burrow and was

relieved to find that he was, at least, still mobile. He could smell Scarface's scent penetrating the hole and he seethed with anger. He crawled painfully nearer the entrance.

'You can wait there till you drop with hunger,' he gasped. 'I will stay here until I die if necessary.'

'You miserable crawling worm,' Scarface snarled. 'Did you think you could kill me like any other fox?' He was intent on discovering if he had cornered his true enemy.

'A violent end is your just desert,' Adder hissed back. 'You will meet it one day, though I may not be your slayer.'

Scarface listened closely. Still the snake had not committed himself. 'You have slain one,' he suggested cunningly, 'but you will never increase your tally.'

Adder remained silent. He was aware he must not reveal himself as the culprit for, if he did, he might never leave that place. At length he said: 'You have wounded me but I have escaped you. *You* can never claim you killed me, however long you sit outside this hole.' Then Adder said no more and Scarface knew that, eventually, he would have to leave the snake where he was.

Still he waited a while, and as he waited he felt more foolish. He had failed to discover who the snake was and, if the real fox-killer was yet roaming free, he was wasting his time here. The day wore on and, suddenly, as softly as he had come, he went away. Adder was left alone in the burrow.

As he lay wounded, he began to plot again. Despite his bitterness against his friends, who knew nothing of his suffering, a scheme entered his subtle brain. He had a new and more valid reason for revenge on his assailant. He had literally been caught napping by Scarface. But when the time was ripe, he would turn the tables on him and avenge this day's work for ever.

—15—
Caught Off Guard

The nightly meetings of Charmer and Ranger continued. No whisper of the arrangement reached Fox's or Vixen's ears, and only Friendly had been witness to it on one occasion when he had stealthily followed his sister's tracks. He kept to his private pact and remained silent. Charmer had no idea she had been trailed. Then one day Fox asked *her* to take the watch for that night.

He had resisted Vixen's suggestion up until then of including Charmer amongst the cubs required to do their duty. Now, after days of quiet, he decided the risk of an attack was far less likely. He believed Scarface had not yet been able to satisfy himself of the connection between the snake-biting and the Farthing Wood creatures.

Charmer gulped when her father made his request.

She was not averse to keeping watch, but she knew there was no way she could let Ranger know she would not be keeping their appointment.

'Could I perhaps take my turn tomorrow night?' she asked hesitantly.

'It's my turn tomorrow,' Fox told her, 'and your mother and I want to hunt tonight. What difference is there?'

Charmer was unwilling to arouse her father's suspicions by labouring the point, so she was obliged to concede. 'None at all, Father,' she answered meekly.

Friendly heard the conversation and wondered if he should meet Ranger and explain Charmer's absence. But that, of course, would be tantamount to admitting his own participation in the affair and that might well have repercussions. So he decided against it.

So it was that Charmer settled herself for the night at a convenient point while feeling concern for what Ranger might think. Every moment seemed an age in the darkness. Behind her, the family earth was empty. Fox and Vixen had trotted off together and her two brothers roamed free as well. She longed for the morning, or at least someone to talk to. She could see no movement anywhere, and the only sound was of the slow rustle of leaves in the night breeze. The night wore slowly on. Then she saw Tawny Owl flutter to the ground from a nearby tree. She called to him.

'Ah, good evening, Charmer, my dear,' he said in his rather pompous way. 'It seems you are our protector tonight.'

'Yes, for the first time,' she replied. 'But there's nothing around to cause any alarms.'

'It's a tedious job perching to wait for something that never turns up,' the bird remarked. 'I really can't see much purpose in continuing these vigils.'

'My father believes Scarface might be waiting for us to curtail them,' Charmer said.

'But we can't continue like this indefinitely,' Tawny Owl persisted. 'We're losing our independence.'

'I suppose he would say that that would be preferable to losing our lives,' Charmer answered loyally.

'H'm. Yes, yes,' muttered Owl. 'But I think Fox is sometimes just a little too cautious.'

'What would *you* do then?' the cub asked innocently.

'Me? Oh well, *I* would go and have a chat with Friend Scarface and see if we could come to an understanding.'

'Of course, we foxes haven't the safety element of a lofty branch to speak from,' Charmer said cheekily. 'We always have to stand our ground.'

'Er – yes, quite!' Tawny Owl said shortly. 'But I'm always willing, you know. Always willing.' He strolled up and down with his wings folded for a moment or two, rather self-importantly.

'Dear old Owl,' Charmer said to herself. 'Always full of suggestions but never carrying any of them out.' She smiled. 'Shall I mention your idea to my father?' she asked out loud. 'Or you could yourself, if you wanted to wait? He should be back shortly.'

Tawny Owl stopped pacing. 'Er – no, no,' he said hurriedly. 'No need for that. I've got to get on. He knows he can always count on me without asking. Er – good night, m'dear.' He rose into the air and flew away abruptly.

Charmer chuckled to herself. 'I shouldn't tease him really,' she thought. 'He's a good friend.'

The smile died on her lips as she saw a familiar shape in the distance, moving uncertainly in a variety of directions. It was Ranger who had come searching for her. Her heart started to pound as she realized the danger that threatened him if Bold or her parents should return. She must warn him. But she dare not leave her post.

The cub came hesitantly forward, stopping to sniff the air and then lowering his muzzle to the ground. He had, no doubt, picked up her scent. In the end Charmer stood up and Ranger spotted her. He ran quickly up to her.

'Where have you been?' he began at once. 'I waited and waited. Then I started to worry so I –'

'Sssh!' Charmer cut him short. 'You mustn't stay here. You're in danger. My father and brothers are out hunting and may come back at any moment. You've got to leave me.'

Ranger looked at her in bewilderment. 'But why didn't you come? he asked. 'I thought some mishap had overtaken you.'

'I can't explain now,' she said quickly. 'I'll do so tomorrow. But, please – go!'

'I met Bold before,' he protested. 'He's no savage. We understand each other . . .'

'You *don't* understand!' she interrupted him sharply. 'If he sees you, there's no knowing what he might do. You're out of bounds and –' Even as she spoke she saw Bold only a matter of yards away, trotting purposefully back to the den. 'Go! Go!' she wailed.

Ranger looked round, following her gaze. But he was too late. Bold had seen him. He raced up and immediately stationed himself in front of his sister protectively.

'I see I returned just in time,' he growled. 'You've come too far out of your way on this occasion.'

Ranger stepped back a pace but made no further move. 'Don't mistake me. I mean no harm. But I can defend myself.'

'We shall see, we shall see,' Bold whispered menacingly as he began to circle round the strange cub. 'Charmer, go back to the earth.'

'No, no,' she cried. 'Let him go, Bold. He came in friendship.'

Her brother paused. 'Oh, what is this? How do you come to talk of friendship with an enemy? What has been going on here?'

'Nothing has been going on,' Ranger was swift to reply. 'You sound like my father. Why do you feel enmity towards me? I've done none of you any wrong. I came to talk to Charmer in peace.'

Bold swung round on his sister. His eyes blazed. 'So you invite the enemy right into our camp?' he snapped. 'This is how you guard your friends!'

'There was no invitation, Bold,' said Ranger evenly. 'Your sister had no knowledge of my approach.'

'Were you asleep, then,' Bold demanded of his sister, 'that a strange fox could come almost up to our earth unawares?'

'No, I was wide awake,' she retorted. 'I saw him come.'

'You *saw* him and gave no alarm?' Bold barked. 'You are a fine sentry, sister!'

'I know Ranger to be no threat,' she explained calmly.

'Oh, and so you would have thought the same if his father had been behind him with a dozen other foxes?' Bold was furious. 'You were put in a position of trust,' he growled. 'Now, how do you justify yourself?'

Friendly now joined the scene and saw how things were. 'Come away a second,' he whispered to his brother. 'There's something you should know.' But what he told Bold only made the cub more angry. He rushed back and leapt at Ranger.

'You'll leave my sister alone!' he snarled, and snapped at the smaller cub viciously.

Charmer ran between them despairingly. 'Don't fight! Not over me,' she pleaded.

It was at this juncture that Fox and Vixen appeared. 'Bold! Charmer! Stand away!' Fox commanded. 'What is happening here?'

'Your daughter is a traitor,' Bold panted. 'She defends our enemy against her own brother!'

'It's not so, Father,' Charmer almost wept. 'I want no one to fight over me.'

Fox and Vixen exchanged glances. Friendly decided to act as mediator. 'Charmer and this strange cub, Ranger, are friends,' he said simply. 'Bold feels they shouldn't be. I believe Ranger to be quite harmless.'

Fox looked at each cub carefully. Then he spoke to Ranger. 'I know you to be one of Scarface's cubs,' he said. 'Is this true what I hear?'

'Yes,' said Ranger. 'I make no secret of it. Charmer and I met by chance and we have become friends.'

'I see,' said Fox coolly. Then he turned to the vixen cub. 'I left you on guard. Is this how you break my trust?'

'But I didn't,' sobbed Charmer. 'I have been at my post all night. Tawny Owl will vouch for me. Ranger was foolish enough to come in search of me, even into such a dangerous situation.'

Vixen smiled at her daughter. 'There's no real harm done,' she said soothingly to Fox. 'I think we'd better hear this story from the beginning. Ranger, you return to your own family for the present. We have some talking to do in our own den.'

'I'll go at once,' he said politely.

'Is he to go free?' Bold cried. 'To go back and inform his father we keep watch for him every night?'

'I want no battles,' Ranger said hotly. 'I shall tell him nothing.'

Fox pondered for a moment. 'Very well,' he said. 'I

shall hold you to your word. You are on your honour.
But if ever I find out you have tricked us, it will be the
worse for you.'

Ranger cast one sad glance at Charmer and turned on
his heel. They watched him go. Then Fox led his family
into their earth.

Some time later, when Charmer had explained
everything, Vixen nuzzled the frowning Fox. 'These
things happen, my love,' she said kindly. 'We never
prepared ourselves for such a turn of events.'

—16—
The Attack

Ranger's father, meanwhile had been brooding over his course of action. The episode with Adder had put him in a very black humour. It seemed to Scarface that every encounter with his enemies ended in frustration. He had not managed to kill the snake and he longed to give vent to his pent-up fury in some way. In his own mind Fox and his friends were to blame for everything that went wrong for him, and he seethed with anger and jealousy. His mate, his cubs and his other dependents kept well clear of him in his latest mood. They expected an eruption and went about uneasily, scarcely conversing, and wished the storm would break.

On the night of Ranger's altercation with Charmer's family, the cub returned to find Scarface's tribe gathered to listen to their scion's intentions. He slunk to the back of the group when his father was looking aside.

'I can wait no longer,' Scarface was saying. 'These creatures are a threat to us all as long as they live. I intend to dispose of every one of them. We will attack them in the daylight hours when they are unguarded. It will be a swift attack, in full force, and those that are hidden will be searched out. I want complete destruction of every one of them, their homes and even their memory. I hope I am understood?'

No voice disputed.

'It is arranged, then,' pronounced Scarface with satisfaction. 'In two days we will assemble here as the light breaks. Now go and strengthen yourselves for the struggle.'

As the group broke up, Ranger wandered off alone to think. His heart told him he should warn Charmer so that, if she felt as he did, at least the two of them could escape the battle, even if it should mean leaving the Reserve. Why *should* they suffer for their parents' enmity? Only *their* lives mattered now. Ranger cared not a jot for Charmer's brothers, nor for her father and mother, and he had no conception of their bonds with the other animals who had come with them to the Park. That was his first reaction. Yet he knew Charmer would never agree to desert her family. She would be less selfish for the future of the pair of them, even if she wished to be his mate. Then, what of his own family? He owed them some loyalty. Could he really be coward enough to run away as they fought for their existence? The more he thought, the more he returned to the same conclusion. Somehow he must prevent this battle.

It would be useless to try and change his father's mind, even for the sake of unity in the Reserve. Scarface was blinded by his hatred for Fox and his desire to be the undisputed authority over the Park's inhabitants with the sole exception of the Great Stag. But what if he gave warning to Charmer to move her family to a place of safety? Yet, after recent events, would she still come to their meeting place or would she be forbidden? If she were not there the next night it would be too late to avoid the collision.

Daylight came and Ranger was still undecided. He felt that many lives might depend on his action, and the full weight of the realization bore down on him. At length he resolved to go that night to the meeting-place and, should Charmer not appear, he must once again go in search of her. Then, worn out with anxiety, he lay down and fell into an uneasy sleep.

It was dark when he awoke and Ranger at once set off in the hope of seeing Charmer. He was quite astonishingly hungry and any likely morsel that crossed his path was immediately snapped up. He was unaware that he had slept a very long time. When he reached the meeting-place and found Charmer was not there, he had no way of knowing that she had got tired of waiting for him and left.

Now Ranger waited, more and more anxiously as time passed. Bitterly disappointed, he knew he would have to pluck up his courage and go deep into Charmer's home area again. But he did not get so far on this occasion. A fox came out of the hawthorn thicket right in front of him, barring his way. It was his father.

'Aha!' said Scarface with a look of cunning. 'Another one testing the lie of the land!'

Ranger was too taken aback to reply.

'Good lad, good lad,' his father went on, not unkindly. 'I never knew you had it in you, Ranger. Up to your father's old tricks, eh? Well, you shall be in the forefront with me tomorrow. We'll teach them all a lesson, you and I. Come on, my boy. Kill me something – I'm starving. I've seen all I want to see for tonight.'

So Ranger was trapped into accompanying his parent back through the area he had just crossed. Even when he was lucky to flush out a partridge Scarface insisted he stay and share it with him. There was no escape. As a final resort, he tried to persuade his father to abandon the attack.

'Must we continue to look upon ourselves as their enemies?' he asked. 'There will be pain and death on both sides.'

'We can't expect to emerge unscathed from a battle,' came the reply. 'My old face bears witness to that. But they *are* our enemies. Yes, a few will fall. But we shall prevail in the end.'

'Why can't we all live in harmony?' Ranger tried again. 'There is plenty of room in the Park for all. We need never come into contact with them.'

'There *was* harmony until the Farthing Wood fox arrived with his conceited cronies,' Scarface snapped. 'But we were here first. The right is on our side.'

'Surely we shall appear to be the aggressors if we attack them? Please, Father, is there no other way?' Ranger begged.

'No other way? Oh yes, we could surrender, I suppose,' sneered Scarface. 'I was wrong about you after all, I see. You're the same cowardly milksop I took you for. Would that you were *his* offspring and his mine!'

Ranger's spirits sank completely. It was hopeless. In despair, he thought of the morrow. Nothing could save those creatures now. But while there was blood still in his

body, he vowed that Charmer should come to no harm —
even if it should mean fighting Scarface himself.

There was one factor in favour of the newcomers to White
Deer Park, quite overlooked by Scarface, and that was
Kestrel. Ever since the slaughter of Hare's mate he had
maintained his observation of the Park by day. High in
the summer sky his piercing gaze detected movement
around Scarface's territory. He dropped height and
found the foxes massing behind their leader. He waited
no longer.

Swift as an arrow he sped to warn his friends. The first
he saw was Rabbit who was nibbling clover with some of
his kin. 'Get down to your warren!' screeched Kestrel.
'There's trouble coming!'

'Is it Scarface?' Rabbit called as his relatives bolted for
their burrows.

'Yes — no time to lose. Is Hare about?'

'Haven't seen him,' Rabbit shouted over his shoulder
as he scuttled for cover.

Kestrel flew on to Fox's earth. Luckily he was lying in
the sun near its entrance. 'This is it!' Kestrel warned him.
'He's coming in force.'

Fox leapt up. 'Right, warn all you see to hide
themselves. Come back to me later.' Kestrel sped on,
scanning the ground. Fox called to his family: 'Quickly,
all of you, off to Badger's set. Tell him the reason and go
deep down. I'll follow.'

With Vixen leading the cubs to Badger's safer home,
Fox loped off to Weasel's nest. In no time Weasel was
following Fox's family to the set. Leaving Kestrel to
search for Hare and Leveret, Fox now thought of the
voles and fieldmice. The little creatures might be safe
enough in their holes but some could be wandering

abroad and, in any case, Fox did not want to risk their being dug out of their tunnels by the vindictive Scarface. He found Vole and broke the news.

'Where are we to go?' Vole shrieked in alarm.

'Badger's set,' said Fox. 'Waste no time. The enemy is on the move.'

'But it's a long way for tiny legs like ours,' Vole squeaked.

'Then start at once!' Fox snapped impatiently. 'You'll be safer there, believe you me.' He ran on to warn the fieldmice, who, fortunately, were a little closer to Badger's home. On the way he shouted to a squirrel: 'Get aloft, all of you, and don't come down till I tell you!'

In the next few minutes, a small stream of mice were scurrying as fast as they could go in the wake of their larger friends. Fox paused, panting for breath. As he did so, he saw Whistler approaching. The heron had seen Scarface's troop crossing the brook and had come at once.

'Thanks, my friend,' said Fox. 'Find Tawny Owl and wake him up. We may need him. But stay well out of harm's reach.' Then he ran off to alert the hedgehogs.

Kestrel found him almost driving his spiny little friends before him in his anxiety to get them underground. Fox and the hawk compared notes. Hare and Leveret had been located and Kestrel had sent them to join their cousins in the rabbit warren.

'I should have preferred us all to be under one roof,' said Fox, 'but there's no time for that now. Have you seen anything of Toad or Adder?'

Kestrel shook his head.

'Well, they'll have to fend for themselves,' Fox said hurriedly. 'I dare say they'll be safe enough.' He stopped and cast about, as if mentally ticking off the animals one by one. 'H'm. All accounted for that can be, I think,' he murmured. 'Kestrel, you've probably saved the day. Owl and Whistler will be waiting for you. Now I must run.'

The last of the mice were entering Badger's set as Fox came racing up. The hedgehogs had overtaken them and, in Badger's deepest chamber, plunged in total darkness, Fox was greeted by his worried friends and family.

'There's one missing,' Badger told him.

'Who's that?'

'Mole.'

'Oh well, he's one we needn't concern ourselves about,' Fox replied. 'He's not likely to surface when he hears all those footsteps up above.'

The animals fell silent as they strained to catch a sound of the approaching marauders. Outside the set, Whistler and Tawny Owl were perched well out of sight in a lofty oak tree. But Kestrel had returned to his natural element – the sky – to watch the enemy.

Scarface, with Ranger and his other cubs alongside him, came cautiously into sight with the other foxes close behind. Everything was perfectly still and silent around them. The fox leader looked puzzled. He had intended to catch his rivals unawares; yet there was no sign of any movement of any sort. Surely some creatures would be about? Then he happened to look up and see Kestrel wheeling free across the blue expanse above them, and he understood.

A crafty grin stole over his fearsome features. He turned round to his followers. 'My friends,' he said softly, 'it looks as though we have some digging to do.'

Ranger looked at his sire in alarm as he saw him directing his band to Fox's earth. Now he must defend Charmer against whatever threat might face her. He ran ahead of the other foxes and reached the entrance first.

He heard Scarface's dry chuckle behind him: 'Oh, are you going to make up for your previous timidity by your eagerness now?'

He entered Fox's den and at once picked out Charmer's scent amongst the others that pervaded the place. He quickly emerged again. 'It's quite empty,' he announced.

Scarface frowned. 'Is it indeed?' he hissed. 'Now where can our Farthing Wood friends be lurking?' He started to look around him and then sniffed the ground thereabouts. 'Oh yes, there's a trail here to be followed,' he muttered. 'Ranger, come here. Your nose is sharper. Lead me to them!'

The reluctant cub bent his muzzle to the ground as directed. A confusing variety of scents assailed his nostrils. Amongst them was one he knew he would recognize anywhere. He thought quickly. Here was a chance for him to lead the wretched band astray.

'Well?' boomed his father. 'Don't just stand there. Track them!'

Ranger followed Charmer's scent for a while to give himself some idea of which direction she had travelled. Then he veered off after a hundred yards or so, losing her completely. For a time Scarface and the others followed in silence. But eventually the old fox became impatient.

'Where are you taking us? We're no nearer discovering them!' he cried testily.

Ranger stopped. 'It – it seems to peter out here,' he said hesitantly.

'Can't you even follow a trail?' snapped his father, bending his scarred head to the path. 'Oh, I can't smell anything! You, come here!'

Another cub's nose was put to the test to no avail.

'Ha! So you've lost it?' Scarface snarled at Ranger

angrily. 'Get to the back of the pack. You're worse than useless.'

Ranger slunk away, wondering what the outcome of his misdemeanour would be. Scarface was furious. 'I'll not be frustrated again!' he swore. 'I'll take some spoils!'

Even as he was cursing, a sort of miniature earthquake seemed to take place right in front of his eyes. A blunt snout and then a furry head, besprinkled with mould, peered out of a hole. Poor Mole, who had heard the running feet above one of his tunnels, had come to see what he had thought was his friends gathering.

'Hal – lo,' said Scarface menacingly. 'You look as if you might be of help.'

Mole jumped. 'Oh! Help? Help to whom?' he cried nervously.

'You're one of the Farthing Wood fox's friends, aren't you?' wheedled Scarface.

'What if I am?' said Mole stoutly. 'Why do *you* ask?'

'Well, you could leave this message for me,' answered Scarface, accompanying his words with a vicious snap at the little creature. His jaws raked the delicate fur of Mole's body and tore through the skin. But Mole turned tail and frantically began to dig himself back into his tunnel.

'Dig him out! Dig him out!' Scarface commanded. 'We'll have one victim!'

But Mole had no rivals as a tunneller and he was soon yards away on the route to Badger's home before his attackers had barely disturbed the soil.

Scarface now rounded on his companions. 'So even a mole is too much for you, it seems? You can't track, you can't dig! Perhaps it's just as well we've done no fighting. You might have had to tackle a hedgehog or a squirrel and then how would you have managed?'

His tribe skulked away from him, looking cowed and resentful. Scarface sneered at them. 'I think you all need a bit of training,' he said. 'Our fierce friends can't stay hidden all day. You'll have to face them eventually. And if any of you have other ideas I'll have you fighting each other!'

Leaving them behind, he went and lay down by himself to wait. 'I've got all the time in the world,' he said to himself. 'I'll make them come out or they'll starve to death.'

—17—
Underground

When Mole stumbled into Badger's set he was amazed to find most of his other friends already there. But he quickly realized the reason for it. He described his tussle with Scarface and Badger jumped up to examine the little animal's wounds. Because of the darkness he had to do this by scent. Mole told him that the damage was only slight.

'How many of the enemy are there?' Fox wanted to know.

'I didn't have time to count,' Mole answered. 'But there certainly seemed to be quite a horde of them.'

Fox looked exceptionally grim but, thankfully, his expression could not be seen in the blackness.

'We'll stay put for the present,' he told them all, 'until

I'm more sure of developments. Does Scarface know of your set, Badger?'

'Probably. He seems to know most things,' answered Badger. 'We're very vulnerable in here, you know, Fox,' he added. 'We have no food – any of us – and there's nothing to stop Scarface coming down here just as you did.'

'We have *one* advantage,' Fox pointed out. 'Our enemies can only come down your tunnel one at a time. So we can dispose of them in the same sequence.'

'But Badger has more than one entrance to his set,' Weasel remarked. 'What of that, Fox?'

'Then we must block all but one,' replied Fox.

'No!' Badger said sharply. 'If we leave ourselves only one exit we could be trapped here.'

Fox thought for a moment. 'I think you had better give me a short tour,' he said to Badger. 'Then I shall know how we're fixed.'

Badger nodded and led Fox out of the chamber. Once away from the others Fox asked: 'What do you think our chances are of defending this place?'

'Slight,' Badger said bluntly. 'All you can do is to post the strongest animals at each entrance.'

'How many entrances do you have?'

'Four.'

Fox mused. 'It's all but hopeless,' he said wearily. 'As a fighting force we are effectively six strong: Vixen and myself, Bold, Friendly and Charmer and yourself. Weasel's too small to be of much help. As for the others, all that can be said is that their hearts are in the right place.'

'I wonder why Scarface chose to come during the daytime?' remarked Badger.

'Obviously he knew about our watch system at night,' Fox said. 'I think I know where that piece of treachery stems from.' He was thinking of Ranger.

Badger looked at him blankly. 'Surely we don't harbour a traitor amongst us?' he whispered.

'Not exactly,' Fox answered. 'But the workings of the heart can blind us to our duty.' Of course, he had then to explain the development of Charmer's friendship with one of Scarface's cubs.

'Goodness gracious!' exclaimed Badger. 'This is one development I never looked for.'

'That's pretty much what Vixen said,' Fox told him. 'Naturally, Charmer trusted her new friend implicitly.' He made a sour face. 'As if I hadn't enough problems already.'

'There's just a chance she might have been right to do so,' Badger observed. 'I think we may be in danger of making Scarfaces of all the other foxes.'

'I suppose there's something in what you say,' Fox allowed him. 'Perhaps I am maligning him. But I feel this raid is too much of a coincidence.'

'You're probably right,' agreed Badger. 'The cub's loyalty is bound to lie with his father.'

'Unlike *my* cub, I suppose?' Fox suggested bitterly.

'Not at all,' Badger declared. 'That's a bit strong, my friend.'

They were silent for a moment or two. Then Fox said: 'I wish I knew what was going on outside.'

'Why don't you ask Mole to go back the way he came and have a look?' Badger asked.

'No, bless him, I wouldn't expose him to that savage's mercy again,' Fox answered. 'In any case, his eyesight's so poor he wouldn't be able to discover much.'

'*I'll* go then,' Badger volunteered. 'I'll be very careful, and I shall know by their scent how close they are. I needn't go outside at all.'

'Thanks, my dear fellow,' said Fox. 'Meanwhile I'll post

someone at each of the other exits.'

Badger shuffled off down the tunnel and paused near
his main entrance hole. Exercising his powerful sense of
smell he turned his striped head in all directions, sniffing
for the tell-tale odour of the group of foxes. Then he went
back to the chamber.

'There's only a faint smell,' he announced, 'so they
can't be very close.'

'Good,' responded Fox. 'But I wonder what he's up
to?'

'We shall know soon enough, I'll be bound,' said
Weasel.

'I'm worried about Hare and the rabbits,' Fox
confessed. 'They won't know what's going on, and we
know how jittery the rabbits are. If Hare can't keep them
calm, they might start to panic down in their burrows and
then they'll be coming out and running all over the place.
Scarface and his tribe would have a field day.'

'Surely one of the birds will come and tell us of any
further movement?' Vole asked querulously. '*They're* all
out of danger. Aren't they thinking of us?'

Fox nodded. 'I'm sure Kestrel will come,' he said
soothingly, 'and, don't forget, you have him to thank for
giving us all the breathing space at the beginning.'

The day dragged on and, just as Fox was wondering if
his faith in the hawk was misplaced, Kestrel could be
heard calling outside. Vixen, who was now guarding the
main entrance answered him.

'Scarface is coming nearer,' Kestrel told her. 'I think he
must have guessed now where you're all hiding. You'd
better tell Fox.'

But Fox was already coming up the tunnel. 'Kestrel,' he
called. 'Please go and see how the rabbits are doing. They
must stay out of sight.'

The hawk flew off and Fox and Vixen peered together

out of the entrance. They could see Scarface now, leading his band towards the set. Amongst them they recognized Ranger.

'So he *is* involved,' muttered Fox to himself. 'Come on, my love, back to the chamber,' he said aloud. 'I'll get the cubs back from the other entrances. Guards are of no use against such an army. Our only hope is to stay completely quiet. We may fool them yet.'

Back in Badger's deepest chamber, the animals hardly dared to breathe. They felt that the artful Scarface would be listening for the slightest sound. The smaller creatures' nerves were stretched to breaking point but, for the sake of all, they tried to hold on.

After what seemed an eternity a scuffling noise was heard, and they knew that one of the enemy had entered the set. The noise came nearer. Fox tensed himself, ready to spring on the animal.

'Is anyone there?' whispered a voice in the darkness. No one replied.

'Charmer? Are you there?' came the voice again.

'Father, it's Ranger,' whispered Charmer. 'Perhaps he's come to help.'

'Help?' hissed Fox. 'He's the arch-villain in this raid. Help? Yes, he helped his father all right, telling him to strike in the daylight. But if he comes any closer I'll make sure he's no help to anyone again!'

'No, Father, please,' moaned Charmer. 'Let me talk to him. He'll listen to me.'

Before Fox could stop her, she had run out of the chamber towards Ranger. 'Here I am,' she said. 'It's me – Charmer.'

Fox rushed after her. 'Get outside before I kill you,' he threatened Ranger.

'You don't understand,' came the reply. 'I offered to be the first to look round here.'

'Of course you did,' said Fox. 'You'll want all the credit for finding us.'

'No! No!' said Ranger vehemently. 'You've got me all wrong. I'll tell my father the set's unoccupied.'

But before Fox could register his surprise at these words, a sneering voice cried down the tunnel: 'The game's up, my friend. You and your cronies are trapped. The set is completely encircled. Ranger, come out! I want no clashes down there. We'll fight them in the open when we've starved them out!'

Ranger turned this way and that, torn between obedience to his father and his feelings for Charmer.

'I believe I've wronged you, my young friend,' Fox said to him. 'Go back outside now. I won't have your father's wrath turned against you.'

Ranger turned unwillingly to leave the set. He felt he was leaving his heart behind him. 'Whatever happens, you have one opponent less,' he told them, 'for *I'll* do no fighting.'

Fox and Charmer went back to the chamber.

'I'm afraid we're surrounded,' Fox said simply.

'We'll die here! We'll die here!' wailed one of the female fieldmice.

'Not if I can help it,' Fox answered her quietly. 'I propose to see just what that scarfaced killer is made of. It's me he really wants dead. Well, he can try his strength against me, but in a fair fight. I shall challenge him to single combat.'

—18—
A Battle

There was an excited buzz of conversation in the set as
Fox crept into the tunnel and vigorously shook himself in
preparation. Vixen followed him worriedly.

'Must you do this, dearest?' she asked him.

'It's our only hope,' answered her mate. 'If we stay here
we shall all be slaughtered or starved to death.'

'But Scarface is treachery itself,' Vixen urged. 'You
can't trust him. Even if he should accept your challenge,
he might set the others on you if you showed signs of
winning.'

Fox smiled gently at her. 'I know you are concerned for
me and, were it just you and me, things might be
different. But I must take this risk for the others' sake.'

'Oh, why must they always depend on *you*?' she

whispered fiercely. But she knew Fox would not be budged.

He answered: 'It was my quarrel in the first place. I'm doing no more than my duty.'

Then she watched him go out into the sunlight.

At Fox's appearance Scarface yapped in triumph. But there was no movement towards him as yet. Only Tawny Owl and Whistler flew to a closer perch, while Kestrel hovered low in the air, ready to swoop down if necessary.

Fox looked at Scarface steadily and then his glance turned to the other assembled throng, who were fidgeting nervously. He noticed Ranger had placed himself well back in the rear.

'You have come in strength, I see,' said Fox coolly. 'Do you need all these to overcome me?'

'You have your followers also,' Scarface growled.

'No.' Fox shook his head. 'No followers – only friends.'

'Oh yes – your precious friends. Well, today they are going to regret they ever were your friends.'

'You have no dispute with them,' Fox said. 'It is me you fear.'

Scarface's eyes blazed. 'Fear?' he barked. 'You talk to me of fear? I didn't acquire these scars by being afraid. I fear nothing!'

'An idle boast,' Fox answered provokingly. 'I say you fear me; and I believe your fear has governed all your actions since I first came to the Park.'

Scarface tensed himself and seemed about to spring on the taunting Fox, who watched him through narrowing eyes. But then his body relaxed again. 'You are clever,' he said. 'I see what game you're playing.'

'Game?' Fox queried. 'I haven't come to play, but to fight.'

The tribe of foxes began to mill about, murmuring to

each other. It was clear their confidence did not match their leader's.

'You are an arrogant creature,' Scarface replied with a cynical grin. 'You would set yourself against the whole pack?'

'Not I,' said Fox. 'Why would I wish to fight them? Only *you* have made yourself my enemy.'

'Oh, so you wish to fight *me*?' Scarface chuckled.

'To settle this issue once and for all – yes.'

'You're a cool customer, I'll give you that. But, you see, the odds are against you.'

'I believe we have an even chance,' Fox replied, 'in a fair fight.'

Scarface fell silent. He seemed to have fallen into a trap. If he should refuse the fight, he would be taken for a coward. He looked up with a grim smile. 'Why do you offer yourself as a sacrifice?' he asked with a grudging respect.

'Because I fight on one condition,' answered Fox. 'If I prove victorious, my friends are to go unharmed.'

Scarface broke into a harsh laugh. 'And all this for a collection of mice and hedgehogs,' he rasped. His face became as hard as stone. 'All right, you have your wish,' he growled. 'And when I've killed you, I'll fight your cubs, one by one, and destroy them all.'

Fox was quite aware of the seriousness of his situation. He had laid his challenge at the feet of an animal more hardened and experienced in battle than any in the whole Reserve. The only advantage on his side was his comparative youth, for he had no illusions about the other's strength and cunning.

The two animals faced each other as if assessing the opponent's qualities. Fox decided to take a defensive stance and so, at Scarface's first rush, he had ample time to swing aside. Then Scarface again rushed headlong at him but Fox dropped flat on his belly, and Scarface's jaws snapped at the air. But the old warrior turned quickly and bit savagely at Fox's scruff. Fox broke free, leaving Scarface with a good mouthful of his fur. The other foxes watched in silence as their leader paused before his next move, while his adversary backed steadily away.

Scarface raced forward again and, with a leap, crashed right on top of Fox, bowling him over and driving all the breath from his body. As Fox lay, gasping painfully, Scarface barked in triumph and, teeth bared, lunged for his throat. But Fox scrambled clear in the nick of time and stood with heaving sides, his lungs labouring with difficulty. From the corner of his eye, he saw the heads of Vixen, Badger and Bold at the entrance to the set, watching in dismay. With a supreme effort he gulped down more air and held himself ready again. Now Scarface came in close, snapping left and right with his awful jaws, while Fox stepped further and further back at his advance. He felt his enemy's teeth and knew that Scarface had tasted blood. They reached a patch of uneven ground and Fox stumbled, his back legs stepping into a dip of the land. Scarface got a grip on his muzzle and held on, biting deep. But Fox kicked out fiercely with his front legs, knocking him back on to his haunches, and then followed up with a lightning thrust at his front legs.

Scarface yelped with pain as Fox's teeth sank into his lower leg and he tried desperately to shake him off. But Fox held fast, pinioning him to the ground and, as Scarface fell on his back trying to wrestle free, Fox transferred his grip to the other animal's throat. To kill was not in Fox's mind but he resolved to weaken Scarface so much so that he would be in no mood for fighting for long days to come. Even as Scarface struggled at his mercy, Kestrel zoomed down with a message: 'The Warden is coming this way.'

Fox maintained his advantage for a few moments longer and then loosened his grip. Scarface lay still, his breath whistling agonizingly through his open jaws. Fox saw the approaching human figure and then ran for Badger's set. Ranger and the rest of the band had already dispersed. The Warden came up to the injured Scarface and bent to help him. As he did so, the animal made a feeble snap at his extended hand, rolled over on to his feet and limped away, his brush hanging in a dejected manner between his legs.

In the set Fox was greeted as a hero again. Most of the animals thought Scarface was dead.

'I didn't kill him,' Fox said as he sat heavily down by Badger while Vixen carefully and soothingly licked his wounds.

'Why not? Why not?' cried Vole. 'Let us finish him off now!'

'The Warden came,' Vixen explained quietly, pausing for a moment in her work. 'But Scarface is defeated. He won't be back.'

'If he recovers he'll be back,' said Hedgehog pessimistically. 'He's as vindictive as a household cat!'

'If he comes again, he'll come alone,' said Fox wearily. 'His tribe's heart is not in this business.' He turned to Charmer. 'Ranger has seen to that, I think,' he added with a kind smile.

'He won't dare to come alone again,' Badger said. 'He met his match today.'

'He has a few more scars to add to his collection as well,' Bold said proudly. 'Father, you were magnificent.'

'Once again, Fox, your bravery has saved us all,' said Weasel. 'But it's to be regretted you weren't able to complete the job.'

'Fox hasn't the killer instinct,' said Vole sourly, 'yet he was quite content for Adder to do the work.'

'It might be as well for us small creatures that he hasn't,' Fieldmouse admonished him, 'else *we* wouldn't be sitting here so comfortably in his presence now.'

Vole scowled at him but accepted his point.

'Let's get back to our normal lives,' Fox said to them all. 'We've been living a false existence. To my mind the threat of Scarface is over. We've skulked in his shadow long enough.'

'Hear, hear,' responded Mole politely. 'He wounded me but *I'm* not afraid of him.'

All the animals laughed at this piece of absurdity and a new, more light-hearted mood prevailed.

'Now will someone please go and release those poor rabbits,' said Fox, 'else they may never come out again.'

— 19 —

By the Stream

It was some days before Adder recovered sufficiently
from his pains to go far from the hole that had saved his
life. He was ignorant, of course, of Scarface's attack on the
Farthing Wood creatures and of his battle with Fox. So
the snake maintained his seclusion in case Scarface might
come again for him. He was not going to be caught
napping a second time!

He managed to sunbathe in complete secrecy, and the
warmth of the sun and what titbits of food he was able to
catch were the best possible medicine for him. His
shortened tail was soon completely healed. This restored
most of his old self-confidence and he gradually ventured
further afield.

It was about a week after Scarface's raid that Adder

came into contact again with one of his old travelling companions. He was lying concealed by vegetation on the stream bank when he noticed Toad splashing about in the water. Now Adder would never have admitted to anyone that he had recently felt lonely and forgotten, but the sight of his old friend gladdened his scaly heart so much that he actually called out to Toad.

'Hallo? Is that you, Adder?' Toad answered, kicking his way to the bank. 'Where are you?'

'I'm over here,' came the reply, and Adder showed just enough of himself for Toad to locate him.

'Well, well, I haven't seen you in an age!' cried his friend.

'No. You don't come up this way much, I believe?' said Adder.

'Oh, I get around quite a lot in the course of my wanderings during the summer,' Toad told him. 'I saw Fox a day or so ago. It seems there was some sort of fight.'

'Really?' Adder replied non-committally, but he was, in fact, greatly interested.

'Yes, between Fox and that scarfaced villain. Fox came off best, I'm glad to say, but not without his share of suffering.'

'Is the – er – scarfaced fox dead?' Adder enquired.

'No, unfortunately.'

'Ah, I'm glad of that,' Adder hissed.

'Glad?' cried Toad. 'How can you say that?'

'Oh, I have an old score to settle,' replied Adder nonchalantly, drawing the rest of his body into the open as he spoke.

'Goodness me, Adder!' Toad exclaimed. 'Whatever's happened to you?'

'Quite a tale really,' Adder punned sarcastically. 'Scarface and I had – er – a difference of opinion.'

'That menace has left his mark on too many of us for

my liking,' said Toad angrily. 'I understand Fox nearly killed him, but the Warden arrived on the scene just at that moment. Apparently Scarface made a raid with his subordinates with the idea of killing all the Farthing Wood animals.'

'Fox was the hero once again, then,' Adder surmised.

'Yes. At any rate, he did enough damage to prevent Scarface from contemplating a second attack. But, Adder, tell me how you got mixed up with him?'

So Adder explained about the cubs' mission to him and how he had bitten the wrong fox, so that Scarface had sought to avenge his death.

'It sounds to me as if you were selected as a sort of weapon,' observed Toad. 'I'm surprised at Fox.'

'It was my fault, to be honest,' Adder admitted. 'I was supposed to strike at Scarface himself.'

'Well, you've certainly paid the price for it.'

'I have. And no one has been to inquire if I am still alive,' Adder said bitterly.

'Then they don't know about your scrap?'

'Oh no. I'm just left to myself, you know.'

'Well, Adder, you always liked to live like that before,' Toad reminded him.

But Adder ignored the remark. 'They *will* hear of me when I've done what I mean to do,' he said enigmatically.

'Er – you won't do anything you'll regret later, will you?' Toad asked apprehensively, wondering if Adder contemplated some sort of punishment for his friends' negligence.

'Oh no. I shan't regret it,' answered Adder with a secret smile. 'I shan't regret it at all.'

Toad looked a little uncomfortable. 'I suppose you – um – don't feel disposed to enlarge a little on your plan?' he asked warily.

'As a matter of fact, my dear Toad,' said Adder

smoothly, 'it's a plan that will be realized in your own natural element – water.'

'Water? Are you going to swim somewhere, Adder?'

'I can reveal no more at this stage,' the snake answered. 'But, rest assured, you will hear it all eventually.'

Toad knew Adder would be questioned no further, so he returned to the subject of the snake's tail. 'I really am most upset to see you in this state,' he said kindly. 'Is the wound very painful?'

'Not any more, thank you for asking,' said Adder, 'apart from the occasional throb when I move. I'm only glad that, like you, I haven't the nervous system of a mammal. I'm told they feel things so much more *deeply*.'

Toad nodded. 'Well, if there's anything I can do . . .' he began.

'No, no,' Adder interrupted. 'Please don't trouble yourself about me. But – er – if you are ever inclined to bring yourself to this vicinity of the Park again, I shall be – er – naturally – er – well, delighted.'

'I shall certainly do so,' Toad said warmly, feeling highly honoured by the snake's uncharacteristic approach to friendliness. 'Goodbye for now, Adder, and – take care!' With a couple of kicks from his back legs he launched himself into the stream's current. Soon he was lost to sight as he let himself be carried downstream.

Adder went back into hiding to review his plan for the hundredth time.

Further downstream Whistler and his mate were dozing on their stiltlike legs in the shallows. It was the arrival of Toad in the form of a soft bump against his leg that caused the heron to wake up.

'Why, Toad!' exclaimed Whistler. 'I might have eaten you!'

But Toad was not fooled. He knew that only frogs,

rather than toads, were palatable to the heron when he could not get fish.

'How pleasant to see you and your charming companion,' Toad said politely. 'You both look in the pink of health.'

'Yes, we certainly cannot complain,' Whistler replied. 'We eat well and we keep out of danger.'

'I wish the same could be said of our friend I've just left,' remarked Toad.

'Who might that be?'

'Adder. He's in a very sorry state.'

Whistler looked puzzled. 'I'm surprised to hear that,' he said. 'But do explain, Toad.'

So, just as Toad had related the details of Fox's fight with Scarface to the snake, he now described Adder's unfortunate encounter.

Whistler listened with a look of concern. 'I deeply regret the fact that no one's been near him,' he said afterwards. 'I, for one, would certainly have done so had I known he was close at hand – and hurt into the bargain.'

'Well,' said Toad, 'I never expected to say this of Adder, but I think his feelings have been more hurt by Scarface than his body.'

'I shall go and see Fox and the others and get them all to atone for their neglect,' said the heron.

Toad thought for a moment. 'No, I wouldn't do that,' he advised. 'Adder won't take kindly to a mass demonstration of sympathy. It would only embarrass him.'

'Yes, I see,' said Whistler. 'But he wouldn't object, I hope, if I paid him a visit?'

'I'm sure he wouldn't,' said Toad. 'But it may not be easy to find him. He's got some important idea he's mulling over and he is keeping himself to himself.'

After a pause Whistler observed: 'You know that Scarface has been more of a threat to us all than the rest of the animals in the Park put together. He's killed or wounded quite a number of our community. While he remains alive he remains a threat.'

'If only Fox had been able to remove that threat,' Toad said feelingly.

'Yes, I fear we haven't seen the last of him,' Whistler replied in his lugubrious tones. 'Oh, I'm sure if more of you had done what I have, we shouldn't have experienced all this trouble!'

'What do you mean – paired ourselves off?' enquired Toad.

'Exactly. If more of us could have mated with those already in the Park – why, there would have been no need for these imaginary barriers and boundaries that seem to exist. But I beg your pardon, Toad, I'm forgetting – you *did* find a partner, didn't you?'

'Yes – Paddock,' Toad answered, smiling a little self-consciously.

'But where is she now? Have you deserted her?'

'Oh, we amphibians only come together in the spring,' Toad explained. 'Once the females have left their spawn in the water we go our separate ways. But that's not to say we won't meet again next year,' he added mischievously.

Whistler laughed. 'Well, I think I prefer a more long-lasting relationship,' he said. 'But – each of us to our own, I suppose, Toad.'

'Yes, indeed,' he replied. 'But there's a lot in what you say and, while we're on the subject of romance, I hear from Fox that Charmer has attracted some interest from a cub in the enemy camp.'

'Is that so?' Whistler shook his head as he pondered Toad's words. 'Well,' he said, 'if that develops it might, perhaps, hold some hope for us all in the future.'

—20—

The Next Generation

The 'romance' that Toad had referred to was certainly developing and now Fox and Vixen encouraged it. After Ranger's sensitivity at his father's attack on the Farthing Wood creatures, Fox had learnt more from Charmer of how he had tried to forestall Scarface's aggressive intentions.

The two cubs now hunted together nightly and in this way news from each camp was exchanged and spread around. Ranger reported on his father's recovery and the opinions current amongst his other relatives, while Charmer told him of the feelings of her own friends. It seemed that neither side wanted a renewal of hostilities, but the one unknown factor was Scarface himself.

'What mood is your father in?' Charmer asked one

night when Ranger had told her he was moving about again.

'He's very quiet,' he answered. 'Almost subdued. My mother has had to catch him his food and I think he feels degraded. He must have hated being so helpless.'

'He ought to be grateful to her,' Charmer retorted.

Ranger smiled thinly. 'Gratitude is not in my father's line of behaviour,' he answered. 'It's more than likely he feels resentment.'

'Does anyone dare to tell *him* how they feel?' she asked.

'Not as yet,' Ranger admitted a little shamefacedly. 'But I know he would never be able to organize an attack again.'

'That's good news anyway,'

'But I'm afraid you can't rule out his doing something on his own when he's out and about again.'

Charmer smiled to herself. 'What a difference between your father and mine,' she murmured. 'Scarface would never have spared my father if he had had the advantage in that fight.'

Ranger shook his head sadly. 'I can't deny it,' he said. 'Oh, I'm so tired of all this!' he cried suddenly. 'Why can't we just live our own life?'

'But we can,' said Charmer sweetly. 'What's to stop us?'

'Oh, he'd cause trouble for us,' Ranger said angrily. 'Can you see him allowing me to choose for my mate a cub of his enemy's?'

'I don't see how he could stop you,' Charmer answered. 'The Reserve is large and we could make our home well away from any other creature.'

'Wherever it was, it wouldn't be far enough away,' Ranger said bitterly. 'We'd have to go right outside the Park boundaries.'

'If it should prove necessary, then so be it,' said Charmer.

Ranger looked at her in astonishment. 'Do you mean that?' he asked her.

'Of course. My future lies with you.'

'Then when shall we go?' he cried.

'We don't yet know if it will be necessary,' she said smoothly. 'Let's be patient.'

They walked together through the woodland, a cool night breeze caressing their fur and murmuring softly to itself in the tree-tops. The Park seemed so peaceful to them then.

'It would be a shame to leave the place we were both born in,' Charmer said presently. 'Perhaps we're getting too pessimistic.'

'I'd like to think so,' answered her admirer. 'It would be nice to bring a third generation into the world here.'

They passed out of the wood into the open grassland. The White Deer herd roamed, ghostlike, through the foreground. The Great Stag stood alone on a slight rise, his graceful neck stretched upward as he browsed from a willow tree. He turned his head slowly as he detected the two fox cubs, now very nearly fully grown, moving towards him. He spoke to them.

'You make a heartening sight after the conflicts this Park has seen recently,' he said. 'Let your generation not recall the ill feeling of their predecessors.'

Ranger and Charmer exchanged affectionate glances. 'We see no reason to carry on the quarrel,' said the male cub.

'Very sensible,' nodded the Stag. 'This Park was reserved as a quiet haven by humans for wild creatures. It would be a pity to destroy their ideals.'

'Your words would carry more weight if delivered to my father,' Ranger said with remarkable honesty. 'For months he's been possessed by a consuming jealousy that has caught up many other creatures against their

will, and I'm afraid it's blinding him to any other
consideration.'

'I shall see if I can speak to him,' the Great Stag offered.
'In the meantime I wish you both well.'

The two foxes ran on, joyful in each other's company.
For the present, anyway, they were able to enjoy the
freedom of the Park. They raced together across the open
expanse, exulting in the looseness of their young limbs.
Then they chased each other in and out of the bracken,
calling to each other excitedly.

Some distance away, Bold watched their antics.
Despite Fox's change of heart, the cub did not approve of
Ranger's friendship with his sister and he scowled. To
him Ranger was merely Scarface's cub and should be
treated as such. He was privately furious with his father
for allowing their enemy to live and longed for the day
when he could fight Scarface and become the new hero.
Ranger and Charmer ran towards him and he greeted
them half-heartedly.

'You're spending a lot of time together,' he remarked
sourly.

'There's no one I'd rather spend my time with than
your sister,' Ranger told him gallantly.

'So I see,' Bold answered. 'She seems to think more of
you than her own family.'

'Oh, Bold, don't be silly,' said Charmer. 'I can't stay
with my family for ever. Ranger is my future. You and
Friendly ought to find yourselves some nice young vixen
cubs and make your own lives.'

'There's such a thing as a family sticking together in
times of trouble,' Bold said roughly.

'Maybe one way of avoiding trouble would be if you
started to mix a little with my family,' Ranger suggested,
in a way echoing Whistler's words.

'I could never have anything in common with any

relative of Scarface,' Bold retorted.

'Don't be so pompous, Bold,' Charmer told him.

'Can't you forget my father?' asked Ranger. 'We're not all like him, you know.'

'But I remember how you all ganged up on me at his bidding,' Bold answered angrily, 'how you trapped me and stood guard over me. I was lucky to get away.'

Ranger sighed. 'There's such a thing as forgiving and forgetting,' he said. 'Things are different now.'

'*Are* they?' sneered Bold. 'For how long? I wonder. Until your father feels he is fit enough to attack us all again?'

'But, Bold, none of us would go with him next time. He couldn't do much on his own.'

'A fox can do quite a lot against hares and rabbits or – or – moles,' spluttered Bold.

'The Great Stag has promised to pay him a visit,' Charmer said quietly, 'in the interests of all.'

'I'm sure he'll listen!' snapped Bold sarcastically, turning his back. He began to walk away. 'He really paid him heed last time!' he called over his shoulder.

'Oh dear,' said Ranger. 'We shall never get on while this animosity continues.'

'Pay no attention to him,' Charmer said soothingly. 'He won't do anything.'

'He sounds as bitter as my father sometimes,' Ranger muttered. 'I don't understand him.'

'I think he's a bit envious of us,' said his companion.

'Well then, he should take my advice. I've got some lovely sisters!'

Charmer laughed, and Ranger followed suit. 'Oh, let's forget them all!' he cried. 'While we're together we only have to think of each other.' He bounded off. 'Catch me!' he called back.

—21—
Retribution

The Great Stag did not at once carry out his intended
visit, and the delay proved Bold's words to be prophetic.
It transpired that Scarface had only been biding his time
while something like his old strength returned to him.
Then, in an excess of spite, unaccompanied and
unexpected, he hunted the more defenceless Farthing
Wood creatures. Fieldmouse was killed, along with
several of his near relatives, and his cousin Vole, while
having a narrow escape himself, saw his mate and all but
one of his small family slaughtered. The only other
survivor was, unluckily, also a male.

Before the news of the night's killings had been
broken, Scarface had added to his toll, in the early
morning, four rabbits, three of which were inexperienced

kits, and a young squirrel. With a sort of fiendish appetite, the killer had eaten all the dead mice and voles and one of the rabbits, and those he was unable to consume he carried away, one by one, and hid in a gorse patch. Only the body of the dead squirrel was left as a sign, as Scarface returned home.

Since Fox's triumph over him, the nightly watch had been lifted and so, when the dreadful tidings spread to his den he fell into an agony of self-blame.

Rabbit, Vole and Squirrel arrived at the earth in the utmost distress which had an underlying current of anger. Anger at Scarface but, in Vole's case in particular, anger at Fox as well.

'You should have killed him, Fox!' Vole almost screamed at him. 'I *knew* it was wrong to spare him! Now see how I've suffered. My poor family . . .' He broke off, inconsolable.

'You were right. He came alone,' said Bold. 'But the cowardice, the vindictiveness of such a creature doesn't entitle him to live!'

'My life is over,' wailed Vole. 'There are no female voles left. I must now eke out my days alone. And you had it in your power to secure our safety for good!'

'Fox was interrupted by the Warden,' Vixen said defensively.

'No . . . no . . . he's right,' Fox said brokenly. 'I *could* have done it. I could have done it,' he ended in a whisper.

Outside the earth the rest of the community was gathering as the events became common knowledge. Badger came into the den. 'Now he has to die,' he said in a hard voice. 'Let us go and finish the job, Fox.'

'Oh, where was the Stag?' cried Charmer. 'He was to have stopped all this!'

'Scarface listens to nothing but his own evil heart,' Bold answered her. 'I told you how it would be.'

'Yes, yes,' moaned Fox. 'I've become too soft. *I* killed my friends as much as he did.' He hung his head in despair.

'You weren't to know, you weren't to know,' Vixen kept repeating to him, sharing his agony in every degree.

'But I *should* have known,' he muttered. 'It was my duty. Oh, that wicked, wicked creature!' He stumbled out into the open air, followed by the others. All the rest of the animals were there, save for Adder. Even Toad was among them.

'Weren't *you* anywhere around, Owl?' Rabbit demanded. 'Couldn't you have done something?'

Tawny Owl resettled his wings and looked away uncomfortably. 'Er – no,' he said. 'I'm afraid I was in another quarter.'

'What protection have we, then?' shrilled Vole. 'We're sitting targets, it seems!'

'Well, you see, Vole,' Tawny Owl muttered apologetically, 'I – er – naturally don't hunt on my own home front, so to speak. Accidents might occur and – well, the sentry duty seemed to have been lifted –'

'Accidents!' broke in Squirrel. 'How would you describe these killings then?'

'They certainly weren't accidents, Squirrel,' said Hedgehog. 'This was planned vindictiveness. I knew this might happen . . .'

'Who cares what you know?' snapped Vole. 'All the warnings in the world have had no effect.'

'I suppose anything I do is too late now,' whispered Fox. 'I can't bring those poor dead creatures back. But will you let me try to make atonement?' He looked beseechingly at the three bereaved animals. 'I'd like to go alone,' he said, and everyone knew what he was referring to. 'No danger must attach to any of you again – not now . . .'

There was a stirring of sympathy for Fox at these words and Mole, typically, started to sob.

'We've *all* suffered for the loss of any one of us,' said Hare. 'The blame can't be put on any one animal's shoulders.'

'Quite right,' said Weasel. 'Why should Fox put himself in this position? We are in danger of forgetting that he and Vixen were the first to be deprived of a member of their family.'

'In my opinion,' said Whistler slowly, 'this whole sorry saga might never have taken place if we hadn't isolated ourselves in the first place. We came to live in the Reserve. We should have mingled more with those already here of our own kind.'

'Wise words, Whistler,' Badger conceded. 'We've made the error of trying to build ourselves a new Farthing Wood inside the Park.'

'Wise words they may be,' said Weasel, 'but wise after the event.'

Whistler shook his head in his solemn way. 'I did recommend you all to follow my example long ago,' he said, 'but, so far, only Toad has done so.'

'After my own fashion, yes,' Toad said quickly.

'Perhaps, then, this is the signal for the future?' suggested Hare. 'I myself must choose another mate from among the White Deer Park does, if I wish to be paired again.'

'There's a lot of sense in the idea,' said Vixen, looking at Charmer. 'We must try and become now, like those who were already here, the Animals of White Deer Park.'

Fox looked at her in admiration. 'Of all now present, I alone found my partner on our journey here,' he said. 'I couldn't have hoped to find a better one in this Park. But my family can be party to this excellent plan and one of them – I think most of you know who – is already carrying it out.'

'Ranger!' said Bold scathingly. 'A cub produced by our mutual enemy!'

Charmer looked at him with pain in her eyes. 'If you think he wouldn't deplore these killings as much as we all do, you don't know him!' she said bravely.

The other animals murmured together. There seemed to be mixed feelings about this proposed alliance. Kestrel seemed to sum up the situation when he asked: 'In the light of Charmer's relationship with this Ranger, who may well have a good heart, how can we stand here plotting to kill his father?'

Fox looked at the hawk pensively. 'It's a valid point,' he said. 'That may have been at the back of my mind when I spared him before.'

'And so *we* have lost our loved ones for the sake of a strange cub!' said Vole bitterly.

Whistler came to Fox's rescue. 'Scarface and his tribe have always hunted here,' he pointed out sedately. 'Lives could have been lost anyway by the usual law of the wild.'

'Yes,' said Hare. 'We rodents must always run the gauntlet of death whenever there are carnivorous animals around. One of my leverets was killed last winter by a creature from the Reserve.'

'A stoat,' said Badger. 'One that I once had words with myself. Yes. One can't go against nature.'

'Then what of Scarface now?' demanded Rabbit. 'Is he still to be allowed to live on?'

There was a long silence. No one wanted to be the first to speak. At last Fox said: 'I'll be advised by the Great Stag. Are you content to be so?'

None of the animals seemed prepared to argue, not even Vole.

'Then it's settled. I'll go now and tell him of the night's

events. He is the acknowledged overlord of the Park. It must rest with him.'

'And how can we defend ourselves in the meantime?' Squirrel wanted to know.

'It's easy for tree climbers like you,' said Rabbit. 'But for Vole and myself . . .'

'Stay together here, all of you,' said Fox, 'while I pay my call. I'll be back just as swiftly as I can. You'll be quite safe in a bunch.'

He loped off, leaving Badger and Vixen in nominal charge. He was not long gone, and when the animals had debated at length what the Stag had agreed to do, they were astonished by the arrival of an exhausted Adder who brought them information none of them had expected.

—22—

A Snake Under Water

After his talk with Toad, Adder had decided it was time to put his plan into effect. In a way he was thankful for his solitude, for it would enable him to act without the threat of interference. But before he could do anything he needed to see that Scarface was up and about again. Keeping close to the stream, he coiled himself amongst the willow-herb and watched the comings and goings along the banks. One day he caught a water-shrew but, apart from that, he ate nothing. Then came the night of Scarface's solo raid.

Adder saw him limp up to the stream's side and gingerly lower himself down the bank into the water. Then, not without difficulty, the fox swam across. Adder watched him limp away with satisfaction. Now he had only to wait for Scarface to return. He noticed the spot on the bank where the animal had chosen to descend, which was less steep than most, and expected that Scarface would try to recross at that point. He slithered down the opposite bank and entered the water.

Adder was a good, but not enthusiastic swimmer. Usually he only swam at all when it was essential to do so. Now he was entering the water voluntarily. At first the current of the stream carried him along a distance, but Adder exerted his strength and, keeping close to the shore, undulated his way back to the crossing point. Then he found a strongly rooted patch of weed in midstream and wrapped his body securely round it, leaving only his head above the surface. In this way he passed the night.

He was very glad when dawn broke, for the water was cold. With daylight it began to warm up. Adder kept his unblinking eyes trained on the home bank, confident that he was all but invisible from the shore. At last, in the early morning light, he saw the awaited figure approaching.

There was a quite distinguishable expression of slyness and cruelty on the animal's face as he looked this way and that around him. He sat down on the top of the bank and yawned, watching the water. For some minutes he sat quite still, his ears pricked for any slight sound. Then he looked across the stream, directly at Adder.

The snake shrank back into the obscuring ripples until only his nostrils were above water. Another few minutes passed. Nothing happened. Adder peeped above the surface again. Scarface was still sitting on the bank, but had his head turned, looking behind him. Adder knew then he had not been detected.

Scarface looked round again and stood up. Slowly, very slowly, he clambered down the bank. Adder tensed himself. The fox waded into the stream and began to paddle stiffly towards midstream. Adder waited, immobile. At the last moment he loosened his grip on the weed stem and, as Scarface came level, gathered his remaining strength and struck upwards. His fangs sank into the fox's soft hind parts under his flank, releasing their full store of venom. Scarface yelped with pain and alarm, but Adder merely dropped back into the water and allowed himself to be taken downstream at the pace of the water. Scarface regained sufficient composure to struggle to the other bank and haul himself clear. By this time Adder was out of sight.

Already weakened by his recent fierce battle with Fox, Scarface lay shuddering on the shore, frightened and angry. The creatures from Farthing Wood had struck back at him again. Were they to be the undoing of him after all? It was some time before he could bring himself to give Adder due acknowledgement for his plan of revenge. It had been masterly and he admitted final defeat. He decided not to attempt to get back to his den. Soon he would die like the younger fox had done. He realized that he had been the real target of his enemies all along. 'Well, at least I've taken some of them with me,' he muttered to himself, chuckling in his throat. 'They won't forget *me*!'

Meanwhile Adder had pulled himself out of the water and was sluggishly making his way back to the scene of his triumph. He felt empty and weak – but victorious. By the time he came within range of Scarface, the poison had begun to take effect, eliminating him from any danger.

Scarface at once recognized the snake's blunt tail. 'So it *was* you,' he whispered. 'The Farthing Wood Adder?'

'The same,' Adder acknowledged wryly.

'Well, you've achieved more than your brave leader could do,' Scarface told him. 'Perhaps you should change places?' He gasped as the first tremors began to shake his body.

Adder watched him without emotion. 'You've got no more than you deserved,' was all he said.

'Maybe,' Scarface answered hoarsely. 'That's the way of things.' He trembled more violently. 'You've – killed – me,' he panted, 'but – remember . . .' He drew a deep, racking breath. 'I'm not – the end of – my line . . .' His words were expelled painfully and harshly from his lips. They were his last.

Adder stayed no longer. The threat implied by Scarface went unheeded by the snake. He was quite satisfied with the end of Scarface. He swam back across the stream and at once set off on the long journey towards his old friends, to bring them the news. It proved to be as well that he did so.

On his way back through the Reserve he nearly wriggled directly under the massive hooves of the Great Stag.

'Take care, my friend,' cautioned the leader of the White Deer.

'Some of us have our eyes rather closer to the ground,' Adder answered irritably. 'We can't look up at the sky like you do.'

'Quite so, quite so,' said the Stag good humouredly. 'You seem to be in something of a hurry?'

'Perhaps I am,' said Adder warily.

'Well, I'm not prying,' the Stag went on. 'You have your own business to attend to.'

Adder could not resist a dry laugh. 'I've just attended to it,' he hissed sinisterly.

The Great Stag looked at him circumspectly, noticing

his mutilated tail. 'You've been in the wars, it seems,' he remarked presently.

'I have,' said Adder. 'But I survived.'

The barest emphasis in the way he answered was noticed by the deer immediately, who already had his suspicions. 'Am I to surmise, then, that your adversary did not?' he asked penetratingly.

Adder's reply was merely a sardonic grin.

'It comes into my mind that you may have saved me a journey,' the Stag observed.

'As I don't know where your journey lies I'm afraid I can't enlighten you,' answered Adder.

'Shall we stop hedging, my friend?' suggested the Stag. 'I was on my way to visit the scarfaced fox.'

'Were you indeed?' drawled the snake. 'Then I can tell you that you will find him quite close by.'

The Great Stag sighed. 'Your caution does you credit,' he said, 'but I beg you to answer a civil question. Is there any point in my continuing on my journey?'

'Er – no,' said Adder.

'Thank you. Now I understand the situation. But you may be concerned to hear that some of your travelling companions were killed last night by the – er – animal under discussion.'

'That news serves only to increase my gratification at what I have just done,' said Adder. 'But who of my friends were killed?'

The Stag told him.

'I see,' said the snake, relieved, despite his recent accusations, that Fox was not among them.

'I hope the Park will now return to its former state of quietude,' said the Great Stag.

'Likewise,' answered Adder. 'And now, if you'll excuse me, I have some news to convey.'

'Of course.' The Stag stood aside and watched Adder

continue on his way. He shrugged to himself. 'Well,' he mused, 'it seems that actions speak louder than words.' He stood for some time looking into the distance. Then he turned and started to walk majestically back in the direction of his herd.

—23—

Loss and Gain

It was not until quite late in the day that the stiff, prone body of Scarface was discovered. His mate, who had wisely never interfered in his schemes, at last decided his absence from the earth was unusually long. She looked for him in every likely spot and, finally, accompanied by Ranger and one of her adult offspring, went to the stream.

It was Ranger who recognized the cause of Scarface's death. After consoling his mother as best he could, he spoke to his elder brother. 'This is the work of snakebite, Blaze,' he said to him. 'The appearance of our father is very similar to that of our cousin who was also killed in this way. It's almost certainly by the same snake.'

'You're very probably right,' agreed Blaze. 'Our father might have been hunting him.'

'I'm sure he was,' said Ranger. 'Some time ago I saw a snake in this area and I told Father where to find him. I thought he had been exterminated.'

'You should have killed the creature yourself,' said Blaze.

Ranger nodded. 'Now I wish I had,' he answered. He had no idea Adder was in any way connected with Charmer's parents or their friends. 'But Scarface was a jealous parent,' he went on. 'He would only have reproached me for doing his job.'

'That's how he was,' Blaze agreed. 'But what now? Any of us might meet the same fate!'

'Then we must eliminate the chance of it,' Ranger asserted. 'I'll comb this area for the culprit, if you go back and round up as many of the others you can. Then together, we must uncover him.'

Blaze led his mother back to her den. She was too stunned to participate in any hunt. Then he returned to the scene of the killing with eight more of his tribe.

'Not a trace of him so far,' Ranger announced. 'We must work quickly before darkness falls.'

But, though they searched high and low, there was no sign of Adder for, of course, he had left the area hours ago. As dusk began to steal over the Park, Ranger and Blaze called the search off. 'We can continue tomorrow,' said Ranger, who was already thinking of his meeting with Charmer. 'We'll have the whole day ahead of us, and we're sure to catch him in the end.'

The foxes disbanded and Ranger made his way to the usual meeting place. He felt no sorrow for his father's death, for there had been no particular bond between them. But for his bereaved mother's sake, he was determined to avenge his killing.

Charmer arrived at the spot, uncertain how to conduct herself. To her parents and all the Farthing Wood

creatures, Adder was a hero. Even more so as he had
narrowly escaped death himself from the very jaws of
their mutual enemy. But she was well aware that the dead
fox had sired Ranger and had, therefore, a claim on his
feelings.

Ranger greeted her in his normal manner, noticing,
however, her reticence. 'I suppose you have heard of my
father's death?' he surmised.

Charmer nodded silently.

'Well, I realize you have no reason to grieve,' he said.
'I've no illusions about your sentiments on the matter –
or of your friends. Scarface made himself your enemy.'

'I'm only regretful on your behalf,' she said to him. 'As
for us – well, there's a general feeling of relief that what
had been an abiding threat has now disappeared.'

'You're very honest,' Ranger answered, 'and I'm glad
you are so. My only concern is that my father died the
way he did.'

Charmer looked down uncomfortably.

'I shall, of course, put that right,' Ranger remarked.

Charmer looked at him sharply. 'What do you mean?'
she faltered.

'We have to rid ourselves of that snake,' he explained.
'We can't allow him to pick us off one by one.'

'But the first death was an accident!' she protested.

Ranger glanced at her curiously. 'How would you
know that? he inquired.

'Adder killed the wrong fox,' she answered. 'It should
have been –' She broke off, aware of her indiscretion.

'My father!' exclaimed Ranger. 'Now I comprehend.
So this was all arranged. You know this snake!'

'Of course!' she replied hopelessly. 'He travelled with
my father from Farthing Wood.'

'And now he's disposed of two of my family,' Ranger
said in a cold voice.

'Just as Scarface disposed of one of mine,' she reminded him. 'And several of our friends.'

'Several?' he queried.

Charmer told him of the recent killings of the fieldmice, the voles and the rabbits.

Ranger fell silent. Then he said quietly: 'That, of course, I didn't know. There's fault on both sides.'

'You mustn't feel vindictive towards Adder,' said Charmer. '*He* was fortunate not to have been killed by Scarface earlier. As it is, your father has marked him for ever.'

'An adder is a strange creature to make a friend of,' Ranger observed.

'There are reasons,' replied Charmer. 'My parents owe him a great deal. He once saved Vixen's life.'

Ranger nodded. 'Then I understand the bond,' he admitted. 'And I am aware that your father could have killed mine had he chosen to do so.'

For a long time the two cubs looked at each other. They seemed to have reached a point of crisis in their relationship. Then Charmer broke away, sobbing. 'If only none of these awful things had happened,' she moaned. 'I suppose it's too much to hope that we should remain unaffected by it!'

Ranger moved to comfort her, nuzzling her repeatedly and licking her fur. 'Wounds do heal,' he said bravely. 'In time all will be forgotten. We should think of the future.'

Charmer looked at him hopefully. 'Are you prepared to forgive?' she whispered.

'Of course,' he replied. Then he recalled the snake hunt arranged for the next day. 'Where is this Adder now?' he asked.

Charmer hesitated. 'I'm not sure,' she answered defensively.

Ranger looked at her piercingly. 'You needn't worry,'

he assured her. 'I won't try to search him out. I'll tell the others I got rid of him myself. They don't know one snake from another.'

She smiled with relief. 'He's somewhere in the company of Toad,' she said confidingly.

'Well, let's forget him,' said Ranger. 'And all the others. Let's make our own plans.'

'Yes,' said Charmer. 'We're of an age to act independently. Bold and Friendly have already left the family home. Once they heard – you know . . .'

Ranger nodded. 'Will they look for mates now?' he asked playfully.

'I suppose so,' she answered. 'At least, I think Friendly will. As for Bold . . . I can't say.'

'Do you wish us to stay in the Park?' Ranger asked presently.

'I would prefer to,' said Charmer. 'I don't know the world outside.'

'No,' said Ranger. 'Nor I.'

'From my father's stories it sounds a hazardous place,' she went on. 'You really do have to live by your wits there. Survival is everything.'

'I imagine the only thing to be said in compensation is that there are no boundaries to your freedom,' he said.

'Except human ones,' Charmer said pointedly.

'Exactly. Well, home is where the heart is. And as long as you are in White Deer Park,' he said gallantly, 'that's where my heart will be.'

'Oh – oh!' she chuckled. 'Now who's the charmer?'

Ranger grinned. 'You make me so,' he told her. 'Now, where do you think we should have our den?'

—24—

A Singular Discussion

The animals' reaction to Adder's news overwhelmed
him. Already exhausted by his aquatic exercise and then
his long crawl across the Park, the snake lapsed into
speechlessness at his friends' wild congratulations. For a
long time he was unable even to explain the reason for
his blunt tail. When he was eventually able to do so, their
excitement was only heightened and, despite their recent
losses, Rabbit and Squirrel joined in the mutual fervour.
Vole alone was unmoved.

When the exhilaration had subsided somewhat he
said: 'This news has come too late for my relief. If
Scarface had been killed a day earlier I should have been
the first to rejoice. However, I'm glad for others' sakes.'

'You must find yourself a *new* mate, Vole,' Hare told

him. 'It's the surest way to ease one's grief.'

'Perhaps,' said Vole, 'and from your words, I guess you are already making moves in that direction. But for poor Fieldmouse even that consolation is denied.'

There was no comment that could be made on this statement and all of the creatures present felt the poignancy of it.

'Let's be thankful, anyway,' said Vixen quietly, 'that so many of us *have* survived. Now we can look forward to more peaceful times.'

'This will mean more independence for us all as well,' said Fox. 'The whole of the Reserve is ours again, to roam in at our leisure. We shall all be as free as the birds of the air.'

Kestrel and Whistler laughed, while Tawny Owl pretended to ignore the remark. For him, it smacked of a certain sarcasm.

'Don't look so straightfaced, Owl,' Kestrel teased him. 'We don't mind a little joke at our expense, do we? Fox knows we've all pulled our weight in this recent sinister business.'

'Humph!' mumbled Tawny Owl. 'I long ago told that Scarface what I thought of him.'

'Of course you did, of course you did, and we appreciate it,' said Weasel with mock solemnity.

Mole tittered while Tawny Owl struggled to retain his dignity. Vixen quickly changed the subject. 'Well, who is going to act on my earlier suggestion?' she challenged. 'The need to integrate ourselves with the natives of the place is now our prime task.' She looked round at the assembled group. 'I'm sure you're all very eligible,' she laughed. 'Who'll be the first?'

'It appears that Hare is likely to be,' remarked Whistler. 'But what of all you youngsters: Bold, Friendly and – you, Mole.'

'Me?' cried Mole nervously. 'Oh dear, I hadn't really thought about it – mating, I mean . . .' He lapsed into a tongue-tied embarrassment.

'High time you did, then,' Whistler admonished him with jocular gravity. 'But, let me see – Vixen, we seemed to be surrounded by bachelors!'

'A bachelor I am, and a bachelor I shall always be, I fear,' sighed Badger. 'Who'd want an old fogey like me? My mating days passed in solitude in Farthing Wood. I was the remnant of the badger population there and –'

'Yes, yes,' cut in Fox, before he started rambling on. 'Don't let's talk of the past. And, anyway, Toad found himself a mate in the delightful form of that plump young Paddock, and *he's* no juvenile.'

'Toad might have a new mate every year – it'd make no difference to him,' observed Weasel. '*We* have to look more carefully.'

'Well now, Weasel, don't be too sure about me,' Toad answered. 'I was rather taken with Paddock, you know. I may just look out for her next spring. But I had no idea *you* had any designs along these lines?'

Weasel gave a little cough. 'Well – er – there comes a time, Toad, for all of us, I suppose . . .'

'Splendid, Weasel!' boomed Whistler. 'Are there any more of you sly dogs around?'

'We rabbits take it all in our stride,' said Rabbit, almost contemptuously. 'We have to keep our warrens well populated, you know.'

'Why?' Adder's lisp was suddenly heard again. 'Does that give you more of a choice for your mating pursuits?'

The others laughed. The rabbits, of course, were notorious for their breeding record. But Rabbit turned the tables. 'What of yourself, Adder?' he asked coolly.

'Yes, my friend,' Whistler joined in. 'When will you allow yourself to become entwined in the knot of love?'

Adder despised this sort of talk and scowled at the heron. 'There are some of us,' he hissed, 'who may not have come to the Park with the sole object of pairing off with the first female of the species he happened to come across.' This was intended as a gibe at Whistler who had named the need for a mate as a purpose for joining in the animals' journey. But he brushed it aside.

'I make no excuses,' he said. 'A solitary life is not for me. But each to his own, I'm sure.'

'We haven't heard from the other birds,' said Hare mischievously. 'Tawny Owl may be a crusty old bachelor, but what plans do you have, Kestrel?'

The hawk looked piercingly into the distance, as if raking the horizon with his powerful glare. 'It would probably surprise you to learn, Hare,' said he, 'that I have had no time to devote to such activities, as long as I felt myself to be the guardian of the safety of you all during the daylight hours.'

'No offence intended, I assure you,' Hare said quickly.

'None taken, I assure *you*,' Kestrel replied, shifting his rather unnerving gaze to his questioner. 'And, may I say, now that my services can, it seems, be dispensed with, that I shall enjoy the extra freedom it will bring me.'

'Very delicately put,' said Weasel. 'But I believe you might have been a bit premature, Hare, in your assessment of Owl. He should be allowed to speak for himself.'

'Well, you know – er – everybody,' Tawny Owl began uncomfortably, 'I must say that I have regarded myself as the – er – nocturnal counterpart of Kestrel – despite what happened last night,' he added hurriedly. 'I'm not very well versed in courtship procedures, you know,' he went on with rather more than his usual openness, 'but Vixen's idea is – er – a good one, I feel and – er – if the opportunity ever should arise when I – ahem! – well, when I might feel so inclined – I – I should grasp it!' he ended abruptly.

The other creatures hid their amusement at his discomfiture, but Adder could not resist one of his leers. 'And I'd always thought,' he drawled, 'that the inclination was necessary on both sides.'

Now there was laughter, but of a good-natured sort, and Tawny Owl was obliged to grin sheepishly.

'I think what I've heard is most encouraging,' Vixen remarked. 'Bold and Friendly, the part you play in my plan will have a great deal of significance. Your sister has set an example.'

'Well, Mother, the family den is too small for us all now,' said Bold. 'Friendly and I must take our chance as it comes. There are wider horizons to explore.'

Fox and Vixen exchanged a glance. It seemed to both of them there was a veiled implication in these words. But they wisely made no comment.

The gathering began to break up, and the two male cubs dispersed with the other animals. Charmer watched them go without a pang. She had thoughts only for Ranger now.

'I hope they follow your lead,' said Vixen quietly, following her eyes.

'Things aren't so settled for me as you think,' Charmer murmured. 'We can't forget that it's Ranger's father's death we've been celebrating.'

'We haven't forgotten,' said Fox. 'But Ranger won't mourn for long, I believe. Scarface was not the best of parents, and I think I'm right in my assumption that Ranger cares more for you.'

'I hope so,' said Charmer. 'Oh, I do hope so.'

'What is equally important,' went on Fox, 'is that there will be no successor to Scarface. He was a natural leader – the others of his tribe are just followers. Such a situation as we've found ourselves in can't arise again.'

'That's true,' Vixen agreed. 'But I have to confess that I sometimes wonder if we haven't ourselves bred a cub with a similarly strong character.'

Fox nodded. He had felt the same himself. 'It's fortunate for us, then,' he murmured, 'that he should include some of our more sensible characteristics in his make-up.'

—25—

Cubs Apart

For Bold and Friendly there soon came the parting of the ways. Vixen's words were very much in Friendly's mind. He had begun to see his quest for a mate as a sort of duty. But Bold had other ideas.

'Shall we take a look around Scarface's old territory?' Friendly suggested.

Bold recognized the reason for the suggestion. He smiled at his brother cub. 'There's plenty of time for everything, you know,' he said. 'The young vixens over there aren't likely to get paired off all at once. I want to see a bit more of the world first.'

'The Reserve, you mean?' Friendly asked. 'Oh yes, it's true there's a good deal of it we haven't been able to explore.'

'Not just the Reserve,' Bold answered impatiently. 'There's a whole world *outside* White Deer Park. Why confine ourselves within the Park's boundaries?'

Friendly looked at him in amazement and in some trepidation. 'You'd go outside the Park?' he whispered.

'Why not?'

'What of all the dangers? It's hostile country out there. Why did our parents leave it to settle here?'

'Hostile!' Bold gave a short laugh. 'It hasn't been exactly amicable inside here recently! And, in any case, if you can go out of the Park you can always come back in again.'

'If you're still alive to do so,' Friendly said pessimistically.

'Oh, don't exaggerate,' Bold said. 'I can't imagine that you're risking your life as soon as you step through the fence.'

The two cubs looked at each other intently. They both knew they had to separate. 'Well . . .' Bold began.

'We will see you again, won't we?' Friendly asked, almost timidly.

'Of course you will, you chump,' Bold answered him. 'I shan't suddenly just disappear.'

Friendly nodded. 'Look after yourself,' he murmured.

'You too.'

They stood a moment longer and then parted without a further word. Friendly went half-heartedly in the direction of the stream. But Bold's steps were eager and vigorous. He sniffed the air and then broke into an easy trot. His eyes searched ahead of him for the Park boundary.

Friendly was overtaken by dusk before he had gone far and decided to catch himself some supper. Bold had been right in one respect. There was plenty of time for this mating business.

After he had eaten, he found himself a spot to sleep. He felt listless and rather lonely. There would be no returning to his parents' earth any more. Even Charmer would be no longer there. She and Ranger would be searching for a new home. He yawned once or twice and then curled himself up head to tail, listening to the night noises. In a few minutes he was asleep.

Bold ran on, exhilarated by his independence. He crossed the Park, running silently through the grazing White Deer herd, to the fence which bordered open country. Then he stalked along its length, looking for an exit. He found a hole and squeezed through it. He paused, snuffling the air, on the threshold of a new world. His ears were pricked to catch any new sound. But he detected no strange scents, no strange noises. He ran on through the night.

Early the next morning, Friendly awoke to see Charmer and Ranger standing over him. He rose to his feet, wagging his tail in greeting, and giving his coat a vigorous shake.

'Ranger and I have been seeking a spot for our den,' Charmer explained. 'We're on the way to look over the area on the other side of the stream. Will you come too?'

'You never know what you might find there,' Ranger added, with a chuckle.

'I'll come gladly,' Friendly said. 'It's new territory to me.'

'Have you seen Bold?' Charmer asked.

'Yes. He was with me for a while,' answered Friendly. 'Then he went off to explore further afield.' For some reason – perhaps a sort of loyalty – he did not mention Bold's intention of going outside the Reserve.

Charmer nodded. 'He's a law unto himself,' she said.

The three cubs arrived at the banks of the stream.
Already Scarface's mate and many of Ranger's relatives
had gathered and were continuing the search for Adder
under the direction of Blaze. Ranger looked a little
awkwardly at Charmer who had obviously guessed their
purpose.

'I'll tell them what I said,' he whispered to her. Then he
called to Blaze. 'You're searching for nothing!' he cried.
'The snake is dead!'

The foxes stopped and looked at him.

'Dead? What do you mean?' Blaze wanted to know.

'*I* killed him,' Ranger lied unblinkingly. 'Last night – I
found him.'

'But how do you know if it was the culprit?' questioned
Blaze.

Ranger thought quickly. 'We had – er – a little talk,' he
replied. 'I made sure before I despatched him.'

For a long while Blaze stared at him. Then, at last, he
said: 'Well, it seems we're wasting our time.' He paused.
'Our mother wants us to dispose of Father's carcase,' he
went on.

'Then do as we did before,' Ranger suggested, 'when
our cousin was killed. Push him out into the water.'

Friendly was watching the other foxes with the utmost
interest. He had marked out one vixen cub as particularly
appealing. He glanced at his companions. 'Why don't we
cross over?' he asked.

They swam across and Ranger assisted Blaze in
pushing the remains of Scarface into the stream. The
current caught the body, twisting it round in a spiral as it
slowly transported it downstream. The dead leader's
mate stood on the brink to watch it go.

'I shall bear no more cubs,' she said, almost to herself.
'I am old in spirit if not in body.' She turned and gave an
appraising look at Charmer and Friendly. 'Well, it's your

life now that matters,' she said to Ranger. 'Times change. For all his faults, we shan't see his like again.'

'No,' agreed Ranger. 'We can be quite sure of that. But come, Mother, won't you return home now? You look tired.'

'What does it matter where I go?' she muttered dispiritedly. 'My life is as good as over. I want no other mate.'

Ranger said no more but led Charmer away from the stream into the area that had recently been the exclusive domain of Scarface. Friendly let them go and began to mingle with the other foxes, edging as close as he could to the vixen cub that had caught his eye.

She seemed to be aware of his presence for she started to look everywhere but at Friendly, in a confused sort of way.

Scarface's mate turned slowly back, following in the wake of Ranger and Charmer. Blaze and the others followed behind her. Then, at intervals, the other foxes broke off from the main party to go about their separate lives. In the end only Ranger's mother, Blaze, Friendly and the vixen cub were left.

'My mother naturally feels aggrieved,' Blaze said, turning to Friendly. 'But my father's death means an end to the fighting and the – the rivalry.'

'I'm glad you see it in the same way,' Friendly replied happily, aware that the vixen cub was watching him. 'My parents named me Friendly and it's in that manner I like to live. The Park should produce no enmities. You were born here. So was I. It's our home and that's all that matters.'

'It is indeed,' affirmed Blaze.

Friendly wished he would go on ahead with his mother. Presently Blaze seemed to sense this. 'Well, we shall probably see each other around from time to time,' he said. 'I don't know where you're making for. But I must leave you now.'

He moved away deliberately, and Friendly felt very grateful.

'My cousin is very diplomatic,' said the vixen cub shyly. 'I'm glad to talk to you.'

'I wanted to make your acquaintance ever since I saw you by the stream,' declared Friendly. 'What should I call you?'

'My name is Russet,' she replied.

By break of day, Bold had travelled a long way from the Park. He felt brave and powerful and equal to anything. In the early morning light the skylarks rose from their grassy roosts high into the sky, pouring out their burbling song. The country seemed empty, wide and challenging.

Bold slaked his thirst from a puddle of moisture and felt a bracing breeze unsettle his fur. This was the place to live. No narrow limiting boundaries for him! He travelled on tirelessly, and it was several hours before he saw the first human. Even then it was only a solitary walker with a small dog – smaller than Bold. The stout cub laughed at the sight and raced fearlessly past the figures with his yapping bark. Why had his parents deserted such a world? Here you could be your own master. He galloped on: on towards the horizon.

—26—
The Animals of White Deer Park

Over the next few weeks the new peace and security of the Park did turn many of the animals' thoughts to other things. They did not seek out each other as they had in the old times and, alone in his set, Badger began to regret his solitary ways. He missed the visits of Mole and wondered where his little friend had got to.

In his dark subterranean labyrinth, Mole was living a new life. He still collected and stored his beloved worms for his appetite was as voracious as ever, but something had occurred one day that had turned his world of tunnels and meals upside down. During one of his periodic feasts, he had heard a scratching noise – a noise of small feet coming, not from above, but from alongside his tunnel. He had frozen into stillness, a half-eaten worm hanging limp from his sharp little teeth. The noise came nearer. Suddenly a hole appeared through the tunnel wall, and another mole's pink snout pushed its way in.

The intruder pulled its body through the hole and spoke breathlessly. 'Sorry to interrupt,' said the creature. 'It seems that my tunnel has sort of led me into – er – your tunnel.'

The voice was a female one, and Mole got quite flustered. 'Qu – quite all right,' he stuttered, nearly choking on the worm he had not finished eating. 'I'm just having a meal. Er – would you like to eat a worm or two?'

'Nothing I'd enjoy more,' said the female, following Mole to his store. 'Well,' she said when she saw it. 'I must compliment you on your choice. I've never seen such plump ones.'

Mole was delighted but tried not to appear so. 'I am known as something of a connoisseur,' he admitted nonchalantly. Soon they were eating together. 'I haven't seen you before,' Mole said.

'No,' replied his visitor. 'It's probably just coincidence. I was born very near here last summer. My parents were killed soon after. I've never strayed far from the area.'

'Well, well,' said Mole. 'How strange. Er – do have another worm.'

'These really are delicious,' she enthused again. 'Do you have a name?' she asked suddenly.

'My friends just call me Mole,' he answered. 'That's because none of them *are* moles.' He tittered.

'None of them moles?' she asked in astonishment. 'What do you call friends then?'

'Oh – foxes, badgers, owls, that sort of thing,' he exaggerated.

'Oh – now you're teasing me,' she protested.

'Not at all,' he answered. 'I'll take you to see Badger now, if you don't believe me. He's my closest friend,' he added a little boastfully.

'How extraordinary!' she exclaimed. 'Don't they try to eat you?'

'Certainly not,' Mole replied. 'You see, my friends are rather special creatures.'

'I see,' she said. 'Well, won't you tell me more?' She was all agog.

'Of course, if you wish it,' he said. 'But you haven't told me *your* name?'

'You can call me Mateless,' she said archly.

Mole gulped as she moved closer to him to listen. 'Very well,' he said nervously. 'Er – well, about my friends.'

Then he told her all about the animals' beginnings way, way away in Farthing Wood, of the wood's destruction and how they had banded together to help each other on their long journey to safety. He might have made his part in the event a little more courageous than it actually had been, but that was only natural. Mateless was enthralled, and Mole was so captivated by her admiration of him that he completely forgot his nervousness, and grew tremendously in confidence.

The upshot was that Mateless never did return to her own tunnel and that was how Badger came to be feeling lonely.

Eventually, of course, Mole could wait no longer to introduce his delightful new friend to Badger, and decided one day that they must pay him a visit. So he led Mateless (who by now was feeling she should have a new name) down the connecting tunnel into Badger's set.

They heard Badger snoring peacefully in his sleeping chamber and Mole went along to prepare his friend.

'Oh! Hello, Mole!' cried Badger, rousing himself, and

very pleased indeed to see the little creature. 'Wherever have you been lately? You've quite neglected me.'

'I must apologize,' said Mole, 'but I've had other business to attend to.'

'Really? What sort of business?'

Mole giggled excitedly and told Badger to wait a moment. Then he went away and returned, bringing a very coy young female mole with him.

'Goodness me! What have we here?' exclaimed Badger, before he could stop himself.

'My new acquaintance,' Mole announced proudly.

'Well, well, well,' Badger rejoined. 'Well I never! Er – enchanted to meet you,' he added politely.

'She's called Mateless,' Mole whispered.

'How extraordinary,' remarked Badger. 'And is that what you call her, Mole?'

'Well, actually, yes, I do,' he admitted, recognizing the absurdity of the name.

'It seems to me, then, that it's time it was changed,' Badger said pointedly.

'What do you suggest? Badger, will you chose me one?' Mateless whispered flatteringly.

'Me? Er – well – er – yes, I suppose so,' he answered. 'I don't know if I'm much good at that sort of thing. Well, let's see. Hmmm.' He pondered, muttering words to himself. Mole waited, anxious that Mateless should approve the choice. Badger continued mumbling. The longer he went on, the more uncomfortable Mole felt, while Mateless began to titter. When he heard her laugh, Badger stopped. He looked round, grinning craftily. 'How about Mirthful?' he asked.

Mole did not know what to answer. But Mateless appeared to be delighted. 'Yes, a lovely name! A lovely name!' she squeaked.

Badger smiled broadly. 'It's more becoming than Mateless, anyhow,' he declared.

'Thank you, Badger,' said Mole. 'You're quite right.' They stood grinning at each other for a moment.

'Er – have you heard news of the others?' Mole asked suddenly.

'I haven't seen much of any of them,' Badger replied. 'As far as I can judge, they're all busying themselves with plans similar to yours. They haven't time really for an old loner like myself.'

Mirthful looked concerned. '*Must* you live alone?' she queried. 'There are other badgers in the Park, I'm certain.'

Mole tried to shake his head at her surreptitiously, but Badger noticed. 'It's all right, Mole,' he said. 'You don't have to spare my feelings. I know your charming young friend is trying to be helpful, but it's too late in the day for me to make adjustments to my life style. I'm afraid I wouldn't take kindly now to another badger's ways – neither would they to mine.'

'We can still come and see you, at any rate,' Mole said loyally.

'Of course you can, and you'll always be welcome,' said Badger. 'But you'll find less and less time for visits as time goes on, I'm sure.' He smiled at his little friend. 'Dear Mole,' he said. 'You have other loyalties now.'

A little later, when the two had returned to their tunnel, Badger left his set to go and talk to Fox. He sensed that evening was falling and he wanted to catch him before he went off hunting.

Fox and Vixen were overjoyed at the news about Mole. 'My suggestion really did take root,' Vixen enthused. 'Weasel and Kestrel have both found mates for themselves, and so, too, has Hare.'

'And Leveret,' Fox reminded her. 'We forget about the younger generation.'

I don't,' declared Vixen. 'Not when I can watch our own family's progress.'

Fox looked solemn. 'You know, Badger, I feel quite a different animal these days,' he said. 'Things are changing so quickly. I don't feel like a leader any more. That whole episode with Scarface changed my life.'

'How do you mean?' Badger enquired.

'It's made me look at myself in a different way. I know that if I had had that fight with him while we were on our journey here, I'd never have spared him. I would have thought of the safety of the party – the Oath we took. I couldn't have let him live. But here, I was always conscious that he had been here before us. The Park, if anything, was more his than ours. So I held back. Of course, I regretted it deeply. I could have saved a lot of lives by finishing him off.'

'Well, Fox,' said Badger, 'it's something that can't be altered. The rabbits and voles – and poor Fieldmouse – can't be brought back.'

'I know I have to live with it,' said Fox. 'But I've lost my self-respect to some degree. I know I'm to blame.'

'You have to stop feeling responsible for everything,' Vixen said. 'You brought the animals here with Toad's directions. You can't live their lives for them now.'

'No,' said Fox. 'But what Adder did – *I* should have done.'

Badger thought he detected a hint of envy in Fox's voice. He was no longer the supreme hero. By way of comfort he said: 'As far as I'm concerned, my life goes on as before. I don't ask for anything except a little company at times.'

'There will always be that available,' Fox answered affectionately.

The three animals watched Tawny Owl flitting from tree to tree in his secret noiseless way. Fox laughed. 'There's another who'll never change,' he said, 'no matter where he might live.' Then Fox lowered his head and looked into the distance. For a long time he stared into the darkness beyond, as if he were watching something far, far away.

Outside the Park, where the evening breezes blew here and there across the open countryside, a sturdy young fox loped over the downland into the enveloping night.

Other great reads from **Red Fox**

Discover the great animal stories of Colin Dann

JUST NUFFIN

The Summer holidays loomed ahead with nothing to look forward to except one dreary week in a caravan with only Mum and Dad for company. Roger was sure he'd be bored.

But then Dad finds Nuffin: an abandoned puppy who's more a bundle of skin and bones than a dog. Roger's holiday is transformed and he and Nuffin are inseparable. But Dad is adamant that Nuffin must find a new home. Is there *any* way Roger can persuade him to change his mind?

ISBN 0 09 966900 5   £2.99

KING OF THE VAGABONDS

'You're very young,' Sammy's mother said, 'so heed my advice. Don't go into Quartermile Field.'

His mother and sister are happily domesticated but Sammy, the tabby cat, feels different. They are content with their lot, never wondering what lies beyond their immediate surroundings. But Sammy is burningly curious and his life seems full of mysteries. Who is his father? Where has he gone? And what is the mystery of Quartermile Field?

ISBN 0 09 957190 0   £2.50